NTS

ABOUT THE AUTHOR

Lawrence Olufemi Obisakin, born 1957, at Ile-Ife, Nigeria, is a career ambassador. He is very versatile. He operates in fourteen languages. He studied on many continents and holds, among other degrees, the following: BA Hons, French, (Ife) DSEF, (Grenoble, France, best result of the year,) BBA, (Brasilia), MA, PhD Conflict Mgt. Indiana, (USA) Dr. of Christian Education, (Georgia), USA. He was interpreter & director of protocol to the Nigerian president (2003-2007.

He retired in 2016 after 35 meritorious years of diplomatic service to Nigeria and the world in: Switzerland, Brazil, Bolivia, Paraguay, Israel, UN, and was Nigeria's ambassador to Benin Republic, 2012-2016.). He was called 'Ambassador of African proverbs' by his United Nations colleagues since 2008.

On retirement, he was decorated with the *Commandeur de l'Ordre National du Benin.*

After retirement, currently, he and his wife, Pastor Dr. Mrs. Cecilia G. Obisakin, serve in Benin Republic, as senior pastors and missionary of The Redeemed Christian Church of God (RCCG). They write, coach, and preach. They also mentor and counsel the youths. He also speaks at conferences on conflict management, diplomacy, and protocol, social and theological issues. They are blessed with adult children and grandchildren

He has written about twelve non-fiction books and two novels.

Cotonou, January, 2021

BOOKS BY THE AUTHOR

Dislodging Demons: A Systematic Approach to Deliverance Ministration. Amazon e-book and paperback editions, 2020.

On the Wings of Time. Ibadan, Nigeria: Spectrum Books Ltd, 2007

God the Holy Spirit, the Mystery of Christianity. Amazon e-book and paperback editions, 2020.

Protocol for Life: Guidelines on Diplomatic, Official and Social Manners. Amazon e-book and paperback editions, 2020.

Proverbs in Communication: A conflict Resolution Approach. Bronx, New York: Triumph Publishing, 2010. . Amazon e-book and paperback editions, 2020.

Nigeria-Benin Border Conflicts: Views Of Concerned Parties, Analysis And Recommendations For Resolution-PhD Thesis, 2013

Managing Interpersonal, Organizational And International Conflicts- Practical And Theoretical Approaches, Ikeja Lagos, Somerest Ventures, 2015. . Amazon e-book and paperback editions, 2020.

Amazing Aroma of love- a novel, Amazon e-book and paperback editions, 2020.

Déloger les Démons: une Approche Systématique d'aborder le ministère de la Délivrance, Amazon e-book and paperback editions, 2020.

For contacts with the author, please write to: lawrenceobisakin@hotmail.com or manofgodfemi@yahoo.com, and also twit him on @divineenvoy.com

APPRECIATION TO YOU FOR YOUR SPECIAL PARTNERSHIP SPIRIT

The author, family and friends are very grateful to the following for their partnership in the realization of this work:
Alhaji Aliko Dangote;
Chief Femi Otedola.

BLURB

Embellished with witty Yoruba proverbs, spiced sumptuously with amazing folktales, and written in the thrilling mode of magic realism, this beautiful autobiography narrates the odyssey of a Nigerian diplomat...

It allegorizes Nigeria's turbulent history of ethnic strife, economic depredation, and political shenanigans; compares communal rural life with desolate city life; brims with wistful memories of childhood sports and schoolboy antics and jokes; and portrays a gorgeous array of charming characters.

... Leaves all insoluble contradictions, mind-boggling confusions, and perplexing conundrums on God's doorstep...

... Nevertheless, the author hands out hope to Nigerians. The book is a pearl.

Prof. Segun Adekoya, OAU, English dept, Ile- Ife.

"He displayed wisdom and skill in articulating the critical societal and religious issues of our times as perceived through the childhood and adulthood of Femoo. Larry Femi takes the reader through the deep affairs of an established community rich in history, culture and educational opportunities...

I recommend this exciting masterpiece to homes, libraries and other institutions because it is, educative, historical, informative, spiritual, and also entertaining".

Dr. Laraba Clara Alfa, mni,.

"The book, On the Wings of Time, is of great inspiration to our youths. The life and times of young Femoo clearly shows that, no matter your social background, with hard work, determination and above all with God, nothing shall be impossible for you to achieve"

Paulette Ukpomwa,HOD, FSTC, Orozo, Abuja

"On the Wings of Time by Lawrence Olufemi Obisakin, like most African autobiographies, is a twice-told story. On the one hand, it tells the life story of the author and, on the other, narrates obliquely the chequered story of Nigeria's political economy.

... cast in the mould of magic realism. Each anecdote closes with an axiom or proverb that encapsulates its moral. Obisakin's novelistic art is best approached as an extension of his pastoral ministry.

The greatest talent displayed in the book is the author's uncanny ability to remember in detail events of the remotest past. Next comes his sincerity.... make reading the autobiography a journey back into one's life.

Another area in which the author excels is the masterful deployment of Yoruba proverbs and idiomatic expressions.

The book contains valuable information on proper grooming, preparing for interviews, making a success of marriage, good professional conduct, and attaining one's goal in life.

A symbolic fable, the author's dream or vision of the Difa gorillas reads like a dark allegory on power play on the political chessboard of Nigeria.

... the author hands out hope to Nigerians. The book is a pearl".

Prof. Segun Adekoya, OAU, English dept, Ile- Ife.

FOREWORD

This hagiography Amazing Adventures of Femoo or On the Wings of Time by Larry Femi Obisakin, like most African autobiographies, is a twice-told story. On the one hand, it tells the life story of the author and, on the other, narrates obliquely the chequered story of Nigeria's political economy.

One of the ingenious devices used by the author is the third person omniscient narrator who is also limited. Although all-knowing, he narrates the story in part from the perspective of a child who cannot comprehend the meaning of some events and adult engagements. A naïve or disingenuous narrator, such as is employed by Camara Laye in The African Child, he removes his mask at unguarded moments and inadvertently reveals himself as the protagonist. Thus, the shifting third person viewpoint is a distancing technique that confers on the work a certain degree of objectivity.

Narrated in chronological order, the plot begins with Femoo's childhood game of building castles in the sand in Ile-Ife, his hometown, runs through his dazzling educational attainments and professional accomplishments, and ends with the return of the protagonist and his family, after a tour of duty in Brazil, to a degenerate Nigeria, the institutions, social services and infrastructures of which are fast collapsing, a deterioration that is the tragic consequence of bad governance and moral depravity. However, the autobiographer's last statement is of hope for the country and the generation of his children. If Femoo, the protagonist, a widow's son, could rise from the valley of poverty, which made him lose classes in secondary school, and clamber to the mountain top where he now comfortably operates, then, all is not lost for the beleaguered country and the hapless generation. Their castles of the imagination, too, may turn in the end into concrete realities.

Cast in the mould of magic realism, the autobiography teems with animistic beliefs and practices, Yoruba folktales, superstitions, and manifestations of the supernatural. Femoo was endowed with the gift of discerning spirits right from childhood, which enabled him to sense in a strange weaver of a basket in the path to a river the power of wizardry. It is little wonder then that he grew up to become a pastor of the Redeemed Christian Church and an exterminator of evil. His first book Dislodging Demons: A Systematic Approach to Deliverance Ministration is a demonstration of how to deal with malevolent spirits. The heavy dose of religious indoctrination had in childhood prepared the ground for his pastoral work in adult life.

.   The greatest talent displayed in the book is the author's uncanny ability to remember in detail events of the remotest past. Another area in which the author excels is the masterful deployment of Yoruba proverbs and idiomatic expressions. It is proof of his long stay with his granny and attendance at elders' meetings.

The racy account of the political crisis that rocked Western Nigeria in 1966, the counter coup that removed Major-General Aguiyi Ironsi from power and replaced him with Brigadier Yakubu Gowon, and the Civil War (1967-1970) marks a significant turning point in the plot. After the war, it has been free fall for the Nigerian society.

The book contains valuable information on proper grooming, preparing for an interview, making a success of marriage, good professional conduct, and attaining one's goal in life. The life of the widow's son is a shining example for struggling youths. Like the proverbial cow that has no tail to drive away tormenting flies, he has sought and found divine favour. He has reached the summit, where he stands before and speaks not with mean men but with presidents of nations. Faith in God and diligence are the secrets of his success. Both the autobiography and its author constitute a sermon on holiness. The work could be interpreted as an extension of Obisakin's pastoral ministry.

A symbolic fable, the author's dream or vision of the Difa gorillas reads like a dark allegory on power play on the political chessboard of Nigeria, where square pegs are rammed into round holes. He thinks that Olusegun Obasanjo's civilian administration makes a difference and gives hope for the future. Abuja, the country's new capital city, symbolizes the vision of hope with which the autobiography ends. It is a vision of scientific and technological advancement on all fronts for humanity. The problematic is how to soften hardened hearts, banish the sway of immorality, and distribute the commonwealth equitably to all Nigerians and all God's children on the planet earth. To perform the miracle, the author seems to suggest, people need the help of the great Teacher who is also the Truth to be taught: Jesus.

Segun Adekoya
Professor of English
Obafemi Awolowo University
Ile-Ife
May 2007

INTRODUCTION

I am honoured to write the Introduction to this well researched novel by Lawrence Olufemi Obisakin. He displayed wisdom and skill in articulating the critical societal and religious issues of our times as perceived through the childhood and adulthood of Femoo.

I admire and respect the author, whom I have known for about a decade, because of his humility and spiritual maturity. Larry Femi takes the reader through the deep affairs of an established community rich in history, culture and educational opportunities as seen through the activities of madam Comfort Yemi (granny), Femoo's parents, his friends, Simi (the housemaid), his colleagues and the community at large to nurture Femoo who turned out to be academically, morally and spiritually sound.

I recommend this exciting masterpiece to homes, libraries and other institutions because it is, educative, historical, informative, spiritual, and also entertaining.

Dr. Laraba Clara Alfa, mni
Educational Planner,
Dep. Director, Strategic Planning (Rtd)
National University Commission, Abuja (1982-2006.)
2007

'The book, On the Wings of Time, is of great inspiration to our youths. The life and times of young Femoo clearly shows that, no matter your social background, with hard work, determination and above all with God, nothing shall be impossible for you to achieve as you soar higher and higher through life on the wings of Time

Mrs Paulette Ukponmwan
Head, English Section
Fed Sc & Tech College,
Orozo, Abuja
5 June 2007

CHAPTER 1
In The Beginning

'Oh my God!'
The elder shouted as uncle Jojo wiped off his glistering face, the beads of sweat. The sun was already hot, but the sky was azure. It was flawless. It was just about mid-day. A few birds were frolicking over the low and brown roofs.
'Jojo, you grab his khaki shorts, or can't you?'
Uncle Gedu yelled at him as he also re-tied his wrapper. He struggled to wipe his pockmarked face.
Paff! Jojo slipped off the concrete gutter. He groaned.
Femoo, sneered, 'good for you!'
'Oh my God! Are you talking to me, you?' He slipped and fell again. This time into the pool left by the landlord's piglets. Femoo stuck out his tongue, smacking his lips. in derision.
They finally got the young boy before he slipped through the gutter hole and head for the street. Mummy held her nose and sighed. She threw her arms up and shrugged.
They dragged him into the big bedroom of daddy. He felt like a freshly caught rabbit from the African thicket. The heavy door locked after him. Rusty trapezium-shaped wire gauze blocked the little daylight from streaming into the room.
Femoo tasted his tears.
They were salty. He smacked his lips in anger. He had wept his tiny eyes red. Hiccups were jabbing his little tommy. It rumbled.
He was hoarse for thirst. He peeped over his unbuttoned shirt, his chest showed how much he had wept. He saw two long trails of dried tear drops,
'But why are they doing this to me?' He yelled, snapping his finger.

1

No answer. He coughed.

He wondered. He coughed louder.

'Mum I know. Her mum, I know too. She's grandma. And I know her very well. She loves me. Oh she does so much. She gives me anything, and I really mean anything I ask for'

Femoo shook his head and patted his Rico hairstyle of those years of the 1960s.

He pinched his right side and sighed. 'But this man that won't let me follow grandma again? Who is he? I really want to know him' He turned these questions over his worried mind.

...and yet, here am I tied to the giant *Iroko* (or hard wood) bed post of daddy!" Musing over his present fate, Femoo could not believe how on earth a father could do this to his son. His tiny 6-year-old left leg, carefully tied with the heavily dyed swaddling cloth, *Oja*, from mummy's wardrobe of African dresses. They all had agreed it was for his personal good. So it seemed.

Femoo, was looking around the room. Everything seemed bigger than him. The bed was as tall and large. The cemented floor had some pot holes in it. Some ants were carrying white crumbs and filing under his free right leg. 'These ants may be tiny but at least they are free' He thought. The bite was like an injection from an uncaring nurse. Curious! He had dozed off in spite of all his serious attempts to punish the silent and uncaring peace of these elders. Until an ant bit him,

Femoo screamed again.

Then, the faded bronze knob turned. The hard wood paneled door screeched. The rusty hinges crowed like the dawn cock.

And in, came a fair tall man in a white singlet over a white wrapper around his waist. It was *kente* yarn with a heavy bulging knot. The lower side of the wrapper was decorated with tassels. He recalled seeing them at the *Igbira* or *Okene* loom on the way to their church. They are forever weaving come rain, come shine in the abandoned house. Not that abandoned, really as Mama *Ololo,* the shriveled septuagenarian widow was there, always talking to herself. She had on, a thick old velvet wrapper, just hanging a scanty old blouse over her withered breasts. Her middle hair was bald for carrying heavy flat stones, daily.

Femoo squeezed his eyes and looked up as a cat siting a rat. He recognized his face. He wears a capital letter E turned on its back on each cheek. And beneath these facial marks were two other lines...scars.

Femi tried to scream again, but... Sh....sh...he swallowed the doubts. Mum said he's daddy! 'This man is daddy?' He wondered and screamed out, 'Me, I want granny...yes gi'me my granny...you can't take granny from me.no, no, no. I want granny, now!'

'You like to what? Are you still crying there? Will you shut up, there!' Dad bellowed with a straight finger across his lips to stress his order.

'But daddy, please, please. I like to... Oh my God...Jesus Christ of Nazareth...

Daddy had something else behind his back.

What? A cane!' His tiny heart skipped.

'You like to what?

Now, let me tell you, you can't follow granny today' Dad said, bending towards his tied up leg. He was loosed.

Femoo couldn't wait, he jumped, screaming, 'so, can I go tomorrow?'

Dad shook his head and smiled at him, exposing a gap. 'You see my son, let me tell you something...you need to start school. In fact, we asked granny to bring you for that'

'And dad, what is school?'

'I'll tell you later.' He shook his head and shrugged as the little Femoo scampered off.

3

He jumped on his mother's spring bed. The bed was smaller but the room friendlier and brighter **was**. Light streamed into the room from almost all the windows. He felt tossed to the highest heaven. Dad went back to his bedroom.

He wanted to run out and join lovely grandma.

Was he free? Totally free to...?

Femoo continued to regret his new town life, thinking and sobbing over his losses. 'The farm. Oh the great village life!'

He sighed. He came back to real life. His reality of small hell torturing him here below.

He now recalled again. He had been crying, yelling and kicking. He relapsed into the sorrowful mood. He was indeed like a he-goat reluctant to be led by a fellow male to the African evening market. He had fallen asleep, perhaps when all his solo efforts had received no positive results. Not even a single careful look at him or a second glance at his case. Everyone in his little world seemed to have conspired to lock him up.

'Keep silence! Sit down there, and don't you utter a word! The orders rang again and again. They claimed he was being rascally. Or was just a difficult boy? Why can't he follow granny to the farm? Is it not just about 18 kilometers away? Why can't he enjoy fresh fruits, boiled walnuts, ripe mangoes or even guavas or just fried plantain? He can hear the colourful African song birds in their various natural orchestras do the tunes in the evergreen tropical forest of his fatherland? And what of the sweet communion with his peers on the farm? Oh... the special natural taste of the delicious unripe but mature roasted plantain carefully scraped on the plantain leaf delicately cut and garnished with red palm oil!

Femoo had even lately rehearsed the special designs of his castles on the sand of his grandmother's hut on the farm. Alapata, what a haven of hope and bringer of refreshing breeze! His mother's ancestral farm! Even the mere mention of your name invokes joy and sweet relief like that of the after rain. What other game or fun could be better, after the pounded yam supper usually taken about 5 pm, It was often accompanied by grass cutter or squirrel head in *egusi* or melon vegetable stew.

After the rain, the village drags sand towards the hut of Femoo's granny. All he had to do is place his tiny feet on the sand filled gutter and heap sand over his feet, press properly and gradually slide out the feet. There you are with beautiful castles of sand! If you were patient at withdrawing your feet one or both of the castles might remain. At times they stand till you invite your playmates to behold your fresh achievement. Sometimes the castles stand till you've turned your back on them but by the time your friends come they have already collapsed!

As if to further ridicule your childish hopes, they hold till your friends come but at the moment they would really admire your feats, they give way. Then a war of words would begin. "Who on earth demolished my castle?" Of course who will ever admit to being the last to have eaten with a lost knife? If you were luckier, your imagination could be extended. You could fence the castle, dig a well, and even plant trees…in fact, no end to such a creative genie.

Perhaps the weaverbirds will drop their nests into his sand castle this time just as Ojo had hinted…it seldom happens but it does. Ojo was his close friend but about five years older. His parents are full time farmers. His father, chief Odu was the village head, known as *Baale*. His predecessor, chief Ewa, had passed on about one year earlier. He had lived to over a hundred years before suddenly he lost consciousness. It must have been a red letter day in the village as this incident provoked the unusual.

His son, a manager in town, had sent to the village his black Peugeot 403, to fetch his father, the *Baale*. The centenarian, being carried on a cocoa tarpaulin as a stretcher, had exclaimed that the incredible pandemonium had finally crept into the peaceful village. Who could have imagined him, a svelte, six footer, marksman, the alpha and possibly the omega of about sixty homesteads, being so carried out of Alapata?

Perhaps that's why Ojo stayed on the farm all the time. He had become street-wise; could even set traps for rabbits in the forest and cat fish in the streams and rivulets that meander in and around Alapata. What a lucky chap he is! His father, Odu, is too busy with running of the village and so he won't be bothered about the whereabouts of his last boy. He would have to learn and grow among the large extended family of his father's harem of wives and half-sisters and brothers. For his ageing father, life is a great school and man is nothing but a pupil in it.

'Ojo', what an awe-inspiring name! No wonder, the Yoruba folklore has it that it is because of Ojo's absence from home that enabled the fowl to hatch her eggs. If Ojo were home, he would have smashed the chicks in their eggs. Ojo, the one who summersaults victoriously at the battle field!

Femoo wonders why these adults love to dash hopes, dreams, visions of up and coming folks. He must invest more time in unearthing these mysteries common to the so-called grownups.

Perhaps, he had not just dug deep enough to see that bright and beautiful light at the end of this tunnel. Why does daddy want to condemn him to the big city of Ife? He had actually been trying to understand. Maybe some things are just too big for a child's head to grasp. After all, granny used to say that the elephant's head should not be part of a child's load. Was he now trying to carry such a burden? At the Sunday school he had been well taught that he should

6

honour his father and mother. There was, the tall and strict teacher had insisted, a good and reliable promise tied to obedience. Can he now recall from that great and terrible book of books, the Holy Bible, the exact text that speaks so well about hearing and doing? Maybe the book of Proverbs...but Proverbs...wait... just hold these rushing thoughts, proverbs! Are these proverbs not *owe* the Yoruba ways of advising those who need wisdom?

That's it! Granny, the great and highly respected cocoa farmer, madam Comfort Yemi, at the elders' evening council in the village uses these proverbs as skillfully as she does the machete on her cocoa farm! "But there I go again, proverb, God's book and my granny's machete, *ada oyinbo*(European machete, more elegant and sharper than the home-made type) as she fondly calls it, what have they in common?" Femoo turned these thoughts over in his mind.

As he does not seem to grasp this confusing tangle of adult life. It offers two separate chairs for his little bums to sit at the same time. Femoo quickly tossed it all away. Hopefully, time or space should clear these dubious double-faced clouds of adult life forever streaming into his infantile or is it growing life. Enough of day -dreaming! He just wants to be free... to be on the farm like the birds, the squirrels or the pretty partridges that float and glide on the heaps of Baba David's farms. In fact, talking of the farm, it may soon be the season of harvest of the pupae or caterpillars- silk worms, the larvae of those edible insects! Femoo can't imagine missing them. In their cocoons, suspended on some trees, these larvae are something else! They must be God-sent for villagers: their source of protein. He later learnt that the Chinese make silk out of such cocoon. How he wished his people could sell them too. But why can't they too?

Thank God for small mercies! If you cannot access the throne you can at least accept *eba* meal. Like the tortoise, never worries and never in a hurry.Not every moment is that regimented and rigorously controlled in town as Femoo had feared. His father's landlord, Pa 'Runtan, a retired headmaster had some pigs for sale. The grunting of the boars attracted him to the pen. Pursuing the swine in the muddy pen was quite a fun. There were some adults too who came to watch. There was that old lady fund of invoking the *oriki,* or praise names of the pigs. At last, the animal was overpowered, tied and slaughtered.

The next stage was then with, the landlady, called, mama *onile,* whose duty it was to dismember the animal and weigh it out in smaller portions for sale. Femoo wandered how pork tastes. He can never know at least not until he becomes independent. For now, it is forbidden by God. In his father's church, it is regarded as unclean. The elders in their wisdom have submitted that what a child must not eat he or she must not feel with the nostrils either. But now, he can think in his wide imaginations, and travel far out of the home.

CHAPTER 2

Warriors!

Little Femoo turned and overturned the scenario on the platform of his brittle, little mind. All that he could recall was a group of catechists, (or are they evangelists?) praying prophetic prayers in the mission house.

It was in the Christ Apostolic Church (C A C) mission house, Moore about four blocks away from his father's house. All was within the Church complex comprising the Pastor's storey building, the faith maternity home and the church reportedly built in 1937. Was the Church land not the forbidden forest where the cock of the spirit world used to crow? Was it not there that the trees shed real blood when even the bark was cut?

Was it not the *Igbo Olose* that was the Greek gift foisted on the first members of the Faith Tabernacle intended by the native authorities to ruin "those intruders and believers in alien religion"? But those earlier warriors of Christian faith did not only clear the forest cheerfully, they also sold all that they had to build the church. They then christened the church and by implication, the quarters *'Oke Isegun'*, meaning mountain of victory.

In the centre of prayers was his mother, or rather, his four-year-old brother, Olu. His memory had been hazy. His elder brother, who was six years older, had refreshed his sleepy head about what had happened to Olu. Poor boy! He had gulped down about a cupful of kerosene. Just how did that happen?

It was in those days of revivals in the Pentecostal churches. A powerful revivalist from Okene had come to town and had revealed that blessed water was a cure-all remedy to all seen and unseen diseases. He even said it would grant extra intelligence to children and all students. All kinds and shapes of bottles and even buckets were used to fetch water that was carried to the CAC, Moore, for blessings.

The commonest of the bottles, however was the green star lager beer bottle, about one liter. In their house, the same green bottle was used to store kerosene for the lantern. Poor Olu had confused the kerosene bottle. Immediately after the grace was said, he had outrun his siblings to drink the blessed water. He must have drunk kerosene instead! But was the taste the same or had he been induced or confused by some force to do it?

It was the pay day for ministers of God and they had returned from their various missions to their Moore headquarters only to meet this challenge. They had no option but to demolish this Jericho wall that may tarnish their reputation as members of the "praying battalion." And that they did effectively: they had surrounded the lifeless body of Olu and called life back into it, they walked round it seven times, invoking previous exploits of their saviour and master: Jesus Christ. They recalled how, in 1930, Apostle Joseph Ayo Babalola had raised the dead at Oke Ooye in Ilesa. Also how Orekoya,a gardener from Mushin, Lagos, in Ibadan, had called back to life a four- day-old corpse of a pregnant woman and her baby! Then what is this ant of a request before their mountain-moving God? They were indeed holy warriors. No quarters will be given. "The enemy will not be forgiven. He must be made to vomit all that he had swallowed", they vowed.

This case that started per chance had quickly become a matter of honour...a task that must be done. They must retrieve every bit of life snatched by this spiritual robber. So they assaulted the gates of hell with life ammunition. And soon...indeed heavens replied... Olu sneezed back to life. Songs of praises and shouts of hallelujahs rented the silent night. Another testimony had been born!

What a welcome relief! Femoo had been forced, pushed, or boxed in the ear to accompany nearly all the steps and stages of prayers. As his little head nodded in sleep there was either an evangelist or an elderly relative on hand to warn him not to backslide lest it be confirmed he was a wizard too! It was the worst that could happen to anybody here! May God forbid that. In his short life he could recall seeing already one or two. They are usually half naked or fully nude, bleeding from various attacks, confessing their sins as they roam the streets of Ife. People would troop behind them yelling "Aje! Aje", witch! witch! Femoo recalls granny had warned him at Alapata. People could be given the witchcraft spirit through kola nuts, food, or even be injected with it. So little Femoo must cover himself at all costs and avoid anybody putting such a deadly thing on him. He would stay awake and ward off these evil elements from the courtyard of his life.

It was late into the night when Femoo, drunk and heavy with sleep, staggered back home. Opening the door was impossible for mum and dad. They had banged and shaken the wooden door but the sleeping housemaid did not respond. After all normal efforts were fruitless, dad tried the unusual: he broke the window and entered in. The housemaid was still fast asleep!   Finally, she had to be drenched in cold water before she returned. Her eyes were blood-red. She was more like a vampire. Her utterances, Femoo was reminded, were so aggressive. We later learnt she confessed that she was responsible for Olu's confusion of drinking kerosene. She had offered him at their coven but the witches had rejected such bitter meat because the victim's mum had loved the maid too much for her son's flesh to be sacrificed. Indeed, love is the most powerful of all feelings. So love can even overpower witches? It was much later in life that Femoo heard the details of this love story.

The housemaid called sister Simi had come with her skin full of craw -craw rashes and nobody would hire her. In other words, she was so unkempt, ruffled like one of granny's layer fowls in which an egg had broken! Mum however picked her, pitied her, and treated her in the general hospital. Her fair skin shone back to life. She had been adopted as a member of the family. But did she accept adoption? Isn't it hard for a duckling to roost under a fowl? Femoo couldn't understand all these. How could he? These are, or at least were, matters beyond the realm of small boys. They belong to the domain of those who can speak with the Divine, the Most Holy. So he kept doing his own things the way he best possibly could. Has his wise granny not declared that a child should not be charged with the responsibility of carrying the elephant's head? Why bother a small child with the deep affairs of this world? Is life not food, fun, and flight for children?

CHAPTER 3

A Night out

Baba's house was a storey building called *Petesi*. It overlooked the Church complex. It was painted, stately, unique and therefore outstanding as all the surrounding buildings were either bungalow or uncompleted buildings. Femoo had often wondered how lucky his cousins living there would be. He recalled: even mere passing through its corridors could envelop you with an aura of holiness.

Baba was a holiness- and- faith crusader and prayer warrior. Why would he not be? He had benefited from the healing grace of the Son of God in Ibadan, that sprawling city of West Africa. His house, an evidence of God's power in changing misery to miracle, was close to Church, God's house and within a shouting distance to the school, unlike his dad's house which was remote and farther away from town.

Since the farm fun was receding gradually, this mansion could as well be a solace. After all, the Superintendent General is his uncle. When, one Saturday Femoo and his younger brother were permitted to go and play there with his cousins, it was as if he had won a jackpot.

At last they could see the television set, telephone and hear record player sing. In those days of early 1960s, there were about three television sets in Ife town. His uncle had one of them. One was in the Palace of the king, the Oba, His royal majesty, the Ooni of Ife. They said one was at Oke DO, that is, the Divisional Officer's hill. But Femoo knows for sure, one TV set was in the recreation room of the Police barracks. They could watch mostly Indian films, much love songs and advertisements and plenty of cartoons. That evening, the screen was full of snow, or as they thought, full of house flies so not much could be watched from Ibadan, the first TV station in Africa.

Then, came the rarest opportunity: see the telephone set and may be, God willing, even lift the receiver too! Well, finally, the golden long-awaited opportunity did come. Boye, his cousin, Baba's son, his age mate gave it him. It was a dark brown set. When the receiver kissed his little ears, it produced an electrifying effect. Who could be on the other end?

How should he know or greet him or her? Finally, the secret was revealed. All he could hear was a noise like that of a boiling kettle, like his mum's kettle that boils water to prepare pap for his father. Perhaps no white man was available on the other end. It was agreed.

The telephone conversation that never was, was never a head ache to Femoo. There was another excitement looming large in the horizon of his little life. He will at long last sleep in his uncle storey building! How God does great things: Femo on Peteesi, Ile alaja, But, sh...sh..., the heavens started rumbling and suddenly thunderbolts crashed out in lightning peals. Just like the beats of an angry Bata drummer, the tropical rain pounded the corrugated iron sheets. What? With this cooperation from the above, even the Almighty had forever sealed the likelihood of any of his parents coming to fish him out of this cozy and exclusive nest!

Boye's mum routinely asked if Femo had told his parents that he would be sleeping over. But what does he care about that? He had been too excited to think straight now. Moreover, his parents ought to know that. Is it not Baba's house and is it not his great uncle's place? He was given a thick velvet wrapper for a coverlet just like the other boys and on bed he dived. Jokes, experiences and stories were exchanged unending. What a joy! Usually, it was very easy to sketch a playlet. All boys would wrap themselves in their coverlet and one of them would act a night guard to arrest whoever exposed any part of his body. Any one caught would take over the guard's role. It was so much fun!

The joy of staying in the company of other classmates, boys to relate with and share sweet stories had overpowered his sense of hearing. Had he not been charmed by the shining Aladdin lamp that swiftly replaced the Electricity Corporation of Nigeria's power outage that accompanied any thunderstorm?

'Bang! Bang!' Was someone knocking at the door? It cannot be, not in this thunderstorm. Femo wished it were a dream. It was not. So soon, the unending banging on the door ended his dream. There he was face to face with his mother, drenched and dripping. His father had ordered that he be unearthed from wherever he was and be produced under his parent's roof that night, rain or no rain. Femo, like his other siblings, knows it too well: the fear of daddy is the beginning of wisdom and safety. What pushed him to such a precipice? Was he excited or drunk? He still remembers granny warning his clientele of advice seekers: palm wine bought on credit will intoxicate its buyer three times. The first time is when he promises heaven and earth, just to get the wine from the seller. The second time: when he is drinking the wine. The third time is when the palm wine seller comes to collect his or her money, and then the buyer begins to run from pillar to post.

Oh no! There was hardly time for him to say good bye to the boys. He barely could wave them off. Soon he was being harried home by mum as his clever cat would its game. The distance home should be less than a mile, but it seemed ten miles away considering what awaited him. Or is it what should await him at home? It was his entire fault: he should have sought permission to sleep over. But had dad ever granted such to anybody in his living memory? Oh this life of questions and these questions of life! Who on earth could answer them for little Femoo? If only he had strong wings like a bird to fly over times and places!

Perhaps he would be able to know and see what awaits him!

In the end, after puffing and bragging about dad's lashes awaiting him, there was more threat than thrashing. Like a small rat with his tail in his laps he snuggled down on his mat under mum's heavy coverlet. Around him his siblings, only younger brother, Olu, his three younger sisters Ade, Ayo, and Lizzy were already fast asleep. Lucky ones, some were even snoring while others twisted and turned in their deep sleep. They were probably dreaming, having achieved that rapid eye movement feat so easy for kids of their age.

Moreover, they have not been too adventurous as Femoo. Or, perhaps, was it the age or gender difference, or simple personal disposition that has made the difference among them? After all, Olu is a boy and just about two and a half years between them. At any rate ,Femoo is older and by the African rule, he will soon invoke this right of being called 'brother' by a younger one. That's what he calls his only elder brother, Ilede. But he is by far older than Femoo and capable of shoulder-carrying him to the farm should the push come to shove!

The housemaid slept on a different mat opposite theirs. Actually the space between the two spread out mats served as the only corridor that mum could walk to the sitting-room, called the parlour. At night, the chamber pot was placed there and emptied very early before the morning devotion. That was for the adults to do: another elephant's head beyond youngsters like Femoo.

Daddy's room was just opposite: a much dreaded place to enter even in his absence. The tropical rain continued its drum beats, unabated, on the corrugated iron sheets. Each time the lightening struck and it thundered, Femoo would smack his lips to minimize the anger of the thunderbolt and prevent it from landing nearby. That was what he saw the elders doing; this world is all discovering and recovering.

He soon recovered himself and would count the square asbestos ceiling above and watch out for the fan light where strands of lightening reflect intermittently. How long will this torture last? Now and then some ants will crawl over his laps. Poor beasts probably seeking warmth or crumbs of food to eat and amass for the rainy day like this!

The Electric Corporation of Nigeria, ECN, routinely switched off their power. Soon he was fast asleep and assured that there would not be war after all. Tomorrow is another day; the day will surely break for all to see. He will surely grow; yes outgrow these difficulties and crises. Our people say, no matter how poor parents are, their children will not stop growing.

GREAT SUNDAYS

Sundays were special days in Femoo's family life for several reasons to different persons. To him, there was plenty of rice to eat at lunch time. Also, there were friends, relatives to meet and play with at children's Sunday school. Often, the Sudan Interior Mission used to hawk beautiful posters on mini buses near the Church. These posters carried paintings about the Bible. The one that captured Femoo's imagination was that of the human soul called in Yoruba, "okan omo eniyan". What an awesome thing to see! Inside the heart of man was that terrible being, Satan with two large horns on his head, relaxing with his two wide eye balls open. He usually rested on a giant fork. With him in this heart of an unbeliever were terrible satanic creatures like frogs, tortoise, and bats, the stubborn goat and of course the serpent. No wonder then, even the man whose heart or soul was being showed, looked so worried, dull and clearly oppressed.

When the Sunday school teacher opened to the next page: what a scene of confusion in the camp of these satanic animals! There was the beam of lights flooding in from the beak of the Holy Bird. all these strange beasts and their ring leader were stampeded out? Light must be so powerful

17

that it could flush out Esu, Satan! Little Femoo was taught that if he admitted the Dove of Heaven into his heart, then his life would be heaven on earth. It must be so. Clearly, the man's face is now brighter and reveals some smile.

The third page usually showed a completely recovered soul, calm, quiet and full of joy. The soul had an angel presiding, the Holy Bird inside, with the Holy Bible well opened at the centre of the soul, full of light. Then the man was all smiles. This is how Femoo would like to be.

Sifting pebbles from either 'ofada' or 'alabere' species of rice was done from a calabash after Church. Usually mum pours the rice into a bucket of tap water and bales some out with a calabash bowl, each time scooping a handful of rice from the calabash which is poured in turns into the waiting basin of clean water. By this skillful method, she gets rid of the pebbles too. This ritual will last some thirty long minutes before the great pot is placed on fire, at long last.

Another ritual is to pour the rice into the earthen pot, fill it with water and place it on the earthen three-stand hearth. After a few minutes, the pot is removed and the rice is simply scooped out, leaving the pebbles at the bottom. The pebbles are rinsed out and then rice is again placed on fire.

It was the waiting period that sometimes made Femoo prefered the pounded yam to the rice lunch on Sunday. Once you heard the pounding of the mortar by the pestle, one could be sure that in a matter of twenty minutes, food would be ready. No wonder then, his people say if the pestle pounds its mother, the mortar, it is not for nothing: it is because there is something in between them. This time, from wherever Femoo was playing, he would know that what was between them was boiled yam, or for his people of Ile-Ife, it could be boiled unripe plantain with yam. Soon okro stew with meat, if daddy caught any game would be engaged on Femoo's plate.

CHAPTER 4
School Begins

It was January, 1963.
The harmattan was hash and cold. Lips cracked, Skin
scratched white. Boys and girls, farmers and traders
shivered, gnashing teeth like hell fellows. Everywhere was
dusty and dry.
It was still dark. Crickets chirped. He felt a thud on his left
rib. He looked downwards at the colourful mat. He could
see black shadowy patterns of Islamic tables, crescents and
the cross with hanging Christ in the middle of two
criminals. His brother snored beside him. As usual, naked
as Adam in the garden of Eden.

He struggled to stand up as a mortuary- ready wrapped
corpse. He managed to peep through the crevices of
Brazilian window wooden louvres. From it, in the hot day
time, they used to watch the agama red headed lizards,
counting their nods as a game. Now, he could see glow
warms still tinkling on the overgrown amaranths heaps near
the latrine. May be they were actually not glowing. He
couldn't care less. He crashed back on the mat.
'Wake up Femoo. . He yawned. *Moom*i says you have your
bath now.'
' But auntie Bose, must it be now?. Please, *Oye mu gan ni
o, e Joo'* He murmured, 'the harmattan is really biting very
hard.
'Today, school begins. Did you hear me well?'
Now he understood clearly why he was weaned and
snatched from granny's hand: it was time to start

schooling! Whoever invented this instrument of separation of kids from their sweet home! But how could Femoo dodge this hell-like ordeal? He had to try.

He refused to budge. There were so many uncles around daddy. The closest of them was uncle Afe, his father's younger brother. He was such a cool guy. He wouldn't even literally hurt a fly. He would quietly walk away whenever it was either Christmas or any festive period to slaughter a fowl. He was so caring. Femoo had taught he would be the one to send him to school.

That was not to be! His other uncle, Osu, had been detailed to deliver him to the class teacher at the CAC Primary School, Moore about one mile away from home. There, a year earlier, his elder brother had just completed his elementary education. They dragged and pushed him. It was again like the he-goat refusing to be led to the market by a fellow male. If he were a Billy goat, giving the leash to a female would have resolved the problem. But he was not. Some lashes of cane were soon landing on his well shaven head. Soon he broke into tears and yelled for help. None was forthcoming. The man and earth, it seemed, were in agreement to deal with him. Once in a while he opened his eyes and could see various pupils filing past on either side of the road, heading for school in different uniforms.

What baffled him was that some of them equally in green short sleeve shirts over khaki shorts were happily heading for this separation place called school. Perhaps those ones had no sweet home or at least nice grannies like him, he pondered. Or is it that they get some candies, and other goodies as his great granny will offer at Alapata?

Finally, he was dumped in class one. Soon the assembly bell rang. It was not like the usual Church prayer time. The leader was the headmaster and teachers were to stand in front of their different classes. Femoo refused to join these lines of separation. He was allowed to stay indoors. As soon as the other mates came in, he jumped out.

He had got half way when the so-called senior boys caught him: they had ruined his plans for freedom. Perhaps granny would return from the farm with all the loads of gifts, smoked game, corn cake, called *aadun* and perhaps some half pennies if you were lucky to be the first to sight granny and help carry home her hand bag.

He would shelve the idea of escaping from class for now. Then came the ritual of registration. He had to stretch his left arm over his head and must touch the right ear. Otherwise, he was not of age and would have to go home and eat more for another one year. He had wished for that. No, he was of age. His mum, a teacher, had been too clever to be caught like other illiterate parents of his mates.

The mistress would want to know his father's name. What a scary thing! Sacrilege! His father is daddy or Baba. How dare any *misisi* ask his name? This is disrespecting the head of his home! Some pupils begged in the name of God not to be pushed to utter their father's name while some wept openly. Femoo's hope of returning home as being under aged had been foiled. Now, he could pretend not to know his father's name but that was not to be. Uncle Osu had laid ambush outside the classroom. He emerged to disperse every doubt on Femoo's registration data! The uncle, short, with a pock-marked face, having done his task, headed home. Femoo later learnt that it was uncle Osu's own way of paying back what daddy had done him earlier in life by sending him to school.

But, the school environment may not be as boring as he had feared, he suddenly realized! Soon, it was recess time. Femoo immediately found himself in a sea of friends, or rather likely friends. "What…what, a wonderful world!" he exclaimed to himself. Some of these tiny tots wobbled to him and jolted him out of his dreams.
- "Friend, won't you play with us?" they asked in Yoruba.

21

- "Why not? he shrugged.
- But what kind of play will they allow us to do here at school?" came his salvo of a question.
- "Just running round classrooms", they replied. And off went Femoo.
- "Young boys!" yelled a stern-looking teacher, in a white short sleeved-shirt with shorts and heavy brown hoses decorated with red and blue pens. "But who permitted you to run round just like that?"
Femoo couldn't believe his ears. "Does one need any permission to run round here?"
As this was not time to find out, his new friends were already on their knees, begging. As he was not used to such, he took to his heels and this time he seemed to have succeeded. Oh, no, he was just settling down when it dawned on him that he had entered the wrong classroom. What a timely discovery too! The class teacher who was just re-entering the class was the one that had just crushed their running fun. Femoo was actually the one being stopped. The recess time was over and the tots that started the running game were actually under age and were therefore expected to have returned home.

Thank God, the closing bell had just rung and soon all primary one and two pupils were on the field again for the closing prayer. What a day! What a shock! All in one day, all in one school day: the first day at school.

Femoo was not saddled with heavy slates or chalk. Unlike his mates, his mother, an experienced teacher, was wiser. She knew no writing would be done yet, so she kept her son's school materials at home.

Really, the school wasn't far from home. But why did it look so far while he was being dragged there earlier in the morning? Exactly, it was just because he was being dragged there. It should not have been a strange place at all. After all, it's always been the Old Church compound to which he goes every Sunday.

Moreover, there were so many landmarks on the way home. Just about two electric poles from school was the abandoned, weather-beaten Oldsmobile car. Femoo stared at it, hoping that one day he, like his older siblings, should kick start it. Although the tyres were all gone, the solid steel of the wheel, stranded and sunk into the earth, were concrete evidence of the fatal fate that must have fallen upon this foreign machine imported to his native land.

As he still ogled the car, he further discovered that weeds, mostly of thorny red and white amaranths, had infested the open back. The solid metal work of the manufacturers still resisted about five or more years and seasons of the tropical sun and rainfall. Who owned this car? Why was it parked in front of Baba Lambert's house? Was it his? Questions leaped out of his mind as he journeyed towards home, still on the school side of the road.

On the other side of the road, about two poles further down, was the C-shaped police barracks, painted in cream colour. Each sectional block comprised two flats with corrugated asbestos roof. An average laterite sidewalk passed in front of the blocks. Each family developed its portion as it pleased. Some were lovers of horticulture and so planted flowers. They ranged from daisy of various colours, to croton and Canna Lily.

In the centre of them all was the football pitch at the corner of which was the recreation room. The recreation room would later become very famous with the kids of the area while the football field would also turn to be a place of social rendezvous for teenagers from the Moore area. But just before the blocks, was the detached bungalow. It was the inspector's quarters. It had its own lawn, usually demarcated with whitewashed stones. Very close to it were very tall tropical trees with shady branches carefully arranged, as it were, stretching like a natural umbrella protecting the senior policeman's semi-detached home.

After the police barracks was the cluster of houses among which was that of Femoo's dad. They had moved there about a year earlier. It was quietly nestled behind his richer uncle's. He quietly turned the corner. He was home. It was a triumphant entry. He felt like a hunter returning from his hunting expedition. They wanted him to go to school and he has been to school. Once lunch was over, Femoo started turning over in his mind the pages of unfinished business at home.

The following morning at the first cock crow, and the first call to prayers, he woke up. There was family morning devotion in the sitting -room, popularly called the 'parlor'. Children were encouraged to pray in their own vocabulary in Yoruba. The senior ones would read the Bible passages. Those could be interesting teaching lessons in Yoruba. The big children would do household chores: doing the dishes, fetching water from the public pump at the police barracks, sweeping the surroundings. He was dressed up for school.

The school routine had started: morning devotion, forming straight lines on the field by looking at the neck of the pupil in front of you, chanting songs and choruses that he didn't really understand. However, the melody was easy to follow.

Studies have now started in earnest. Granny had bought for him a multicoloured leather bag made of red, blue, and white square patches of leather carefully sewn together. Or maybe, a bag with a double handles of imitation leather, was the emblem of elementary school pupils of the early sixties in southwestern Nigeria, Femoo recalls. In it were always found: a wooden slate, various sizes and shapes and colours of chalk pieces, pictorial English reader, arithmetic book, a drawing book and a packet of crayons.

All subjects were fun and so were welcome. The English lessons were not too bad. The teacher with her flowing skirt, heavily pleated, was respectfully addressed as *misisi*. If anybody failed to address her as such there were various pains inflicted, ranging from not going on recess and a terrible posture euphemistically called in Yoruba, *Ijoko Idera,* which is, "sitting at ease". There was nothing at ease at all in this. It was an extremely painful posture by which the victims would sit on the floor, backing the class, raising the two legs and arms. Neither of the limbs must rest on the usually cold cemented floor!

If the pupil was lucky he or she could serve the ordeal five to ten minutes, otherwise it could last longer. But thank God, the teacher could doze off while the pupils relax to the admiration of their cheering or conniving friends. At times, in the heat of the scotching midday sun, half of them could equally follow the teacher's example.

Femoo can still recall another swift but painful punishment used by the teachers. By this, the pupils are simply paired up and instructed to slap each other as much as possible. If anyone didn't do it well another pupil would teach him or her how to.

The English classes were highly demonstrative. The teacher would, for example drag out her chair, place a book on it, and exclaim, "The book is on the chair!" The pupils would repeat. She could change the position of the book and yell out, "the book is under the chair!" Pupils who were brave would take turns to act the teacher while the pupils would chorus along. Now Femoo can't remember choosing to lead these choruses. Not that he didn't know them; his mind was simply not on these classes where active boys and girls were locked up for hours. He was either thinking of granny's farm freedom…or the school bell. Oh the bell, beautiful jingles of the bronze bells! They opened the door to recess freedom or lunch brake. Or, better still, they could offer Femoo freedom for the whole day if they were the closing bell jingles. If it was a Friday closing bell at one o'clock, it was like paradise on earth, especially if Granny would be home with lots of fun and gifts to share.

Drawing classes were free for all. Either the crayons or the coloured chalk could run as wide as the pupil's imagination could roam. Everyone got a long right mark ticked on his page. All you needed do was show or tell the teacher what you believed that you had drawn. In case you lacked the words, the teacher would ask you leading questions and all you needed do was to nod 'yes', and there was your big right mark on your work!

The teachers could be innovative! Whenever it rained, especially with thunderstorm, and teaching could hardly be heard, then drawing classes were introduced. If it was not too stormy, then there could be music classes. For less imaginative teachers, pupils were simply told to sleep. Some would snore away, placing their chins on the wooden desks.

For Femoo and more imaginative classmates, it was time to enjoy another world of 'rain music'. How was that? It was simple. Just block your two ears with each of the index fingers and release and momentarily seal the ear holes one after the other. There was the melodious clatter of the rain sounds on the corrugated zinc, making "wen..wen…" Oh Femoo could now recall: there was fun anytime, with anything for the African child at little or no cost: how God does great wonders for small people!

Oh! How Femoo loved poetry! In primary class two, the headmaster often joined all the arms of their class together to teach them either stories or poem recitations. Some of the memorable ones in Yoruba are:
Yi, yi, yi ese re s'apa kan (, turn, turn your feet to the other side)
Kokoro ti iwo ko naani ni (that insect that you value not)
Olorun ni o lee da a   (only God can create it)

Or,

ja itanna ti o ntan (Pick the blossoming flower)
T'o tutu t'o si dara (that is fresh and pretty)
Ma duro d'ojo ola (Wait not till tomorrow)
Akoko n sare tete (Time is flying fast)
These poems were written and illustrated on large posters and displaced in Femoo's class. They were even sung in mornings as matching songs as pupils filed into their classrooms.

But then, arithmetic was the enemy number one of Femoo. Whoever invented this strange subject must be the black Satan with two large horns on his head! At least so he thought. He had one big question unanswered, or rather unanswerable for him: why on earth should one zero (i. e. figure 10) follow nine? Why? Was it not figure one that was carrying zero on its head (i.e., figure 9) that the teacher called nine? Why this fraud of changing names and rules in the middle of the numeral game?

Femoo would not write or copy beyond figure nine. His mind was made up. He would cry and cry as the teacher insisted that he must copy the second line of figures ten to twenty, he made up his mind to escape from this daylight deceit.

How God does his things! His mother was suddenly transferred to another school. Just Providence, or some daddy or mummy changed their mind. He may never know the real reason for the change of school. However it was concocted. The great and interesting truth was that Femoo was in another school in town.

He had hoped to enjoy the change for a longer period but there it came again, this game of counting. His excitement was therefore short-lived. Nevertheless, the new class teacher loved singing lessons and seemed to enjoy his afternoon nap more! Moreover, the school year was coming to an end.

Insect Meals

The new school, situated at the Arubidi district but under the same C.A. C. Church mission, was quite spacious. While on recess, pupils could slip down the slope or play with grasshoppers. Pupils could roll over on lemon grass with its amazingly sweet aroma. He later learnt that lemon grass tea was great for the health.

There was also a great fun on the field called *kokoro wuye, wuye, wuye* that is 'wriggling insect, wriggling, wriggling'. Just how was that done? It was very simple but exciting. A group of pupils would gather dry grass in a big heap on the field, and one of them would volunteer to act the wriggling insect or larva. He would lie down and the others would cover him up with the dry grass before they would start to sing: wriggling insect oh! Wriggling insect! The boy insect suddenly jumped up and if he could catch any other boy, then the victim would act the next wriggling insect.

Femoo could even pick solitary locusts lurking under the broad leaves of the elephant grass, or the tall wild okro plants surrounding the new pit latrines.

One day, Femoo remembers, he was attracted by the six-inch solitary locust. As his father used to teach him, methods were very vital, even in catching locusts too. Their limbs were armed with claws as thorns on rose stems; any senseless rush at them could be bloody. Also these insects were quite tricky: they often spat out of their mouths some horrible, dark, foul-smelling liquid. If a child was not determined enough he or she could lose these golden insects!

There was also the swarm of green-yellow grasshoppers that came seasonally. To Femoo they were nothing but nature's kind way of offering toys to poor children. Until…yes until his friend, Idowu, the Pastor's kid from Ifon, told him how delicious those grasshoppers could be if roasted. But Femoo wouldn't have that at all. He relished the flying termites that swarmed most southern Nigerian cities at night usually after the rains, in June. They are six-winged flying insects called in Yoruba, *esunsun or zinge* in the north.

There were two ways of catching them. You could pursue them at night as they hover round electric or any lamp at night. Usually all you needed to do was to place under the lamp, a basin of water and watch the insects fall into the water. This method has the inconvenience of having to sundry the insects and remove their wings the following morning. This could last the whole day or even two days depending on how much you must have drenched them. There was also the greater danger of unconsciously scaring away the toads who relish the insects.

Toads don't bite. They could croak and puff. The worst they could do to you was to squirt on you their whitish fluid. You may ask, why the danger of toads? Yes, because dangerous snakes also crawl out at such nights to ambush their favorite meal: toads. Unsuspecting children might step on snakes in their hide -outs and get bitten by venomous snakes. In fact, this was the main reason why Femoo's dad would not allow his children to go hunting for *esunsun*, like other boys.

He was a very cautious daddy. Perhaps he had learnt most of these ways of hunting down dangers from his earlier life with the British Constabulary Force, a big name for the Police Force of Britain which colonized Nigeria in those days. Femoo had learnt, from mummy, that daddy was easily the greatest marksman of his time. Actually, it was told him that his father could have been commissioned or converted into the army if he had not deliberately missed one target at the Police annual target shooting contest.

Perhaps life could have held a better hope for the family? Only the Almighty knows.

A less strenuous method of catching these highly protein-rich insects was to wait till the following morning after they must have lost their wings hovering round various lamps. They then crawl, under stones and various objects, on the ground: probably hiding away from other predators. All that Femoo and his friends needed do was to lift the objects and pack them into basins. They could then be washed, if you cared, and then fried. Even sun drying them was often enough before they were eaten as dried meat to accompany garri as a wonderful refreshing drink in the tropical sun. It was the poor man's or student's savior.

Indeed, as the Nigerian people wisely put it, a patient man can cook a stone till it is done! Isn't it also said that it is a patient person that milks a lioness?

Another insect usually accompanied the above flying termites. It is the goliath beetle, called in Yoruba, 'Paripa'. The male had a horn like that of the rhinoceros while the female had none. They could fly alone or in pairs. The flapping of their wings usually heralded them as they took off from the palm trees that dotted the built up areas of the cities. They would also hover round lamps. They didn't shed their wings but preferred to either crawl on the flood or play possum if anybody picked them up.

Femoo used to pack a few of the beetles inside Ovaltine or Bournvita tins well sealed but with their lids perforated to enable the insects to breathe. They were usually grilled or roasted in the open fire, salted and shared among siblings.

Going to school at Iloro was much fun also because mum had arranged a taxi driver to pick her up with Femoo. It was the usual black Morris minor. Whenever the driver failed to call, the five miles could be trekked but that was only once in a blue moon.

Femoo could also recall mum's transfer to another CAC mission school at *Itamarun,* about eight miles away from home. There were occasions, during the raining season, when in the middle of the journey homeward, all vehicles had to park.

This was because the bridge, made of four stems of palm trees placed across the stream, had been covered by flood water. At times, they were simply flushed away by the furious torrent. Everybody had to wait till the flood subsided. Since the village was relatively far, coming home daily was shelved and mum and Femoo had to stay on the farm from Monday till Friday. Of course there was usually a cousin, sister Bose, taking care of the younger siblings' feeding.

It was a good, farm settlement. The village comprised about one hundred homestead. His aunts, uncles, were there whom he had never met before but who apparently knew him and perhaps all about his coming there. There was his aunt, his dad's youngest sister, cousin Emman's mum. She was very kind. Each time Femoo ran an errand to her hut, she would give him three pence. It was much money in those days. There, he also realized that some of his relatives also had cocoa farms in Granny's Alapata village. So Femoo was not a total stranger in this new school place. There came a time when about five of the six teachers were his mum's relations; only the headmaster was an Ekiti man!

The school was a smaller one comprising only six classrooms. It was painted in the typical yellow colour; there was a football pitch in front of the L-shaped block of classrooms. Practically, all the teachers were Femoo's relatives and so Yoruba was naturally spoken, save in classrooms.

The Strange Weaver

Evenings and dawns were spent at the small Christ Apostolic Church parish. However, fetching water at the only clean stream situated a stone's throw from their hut was exciting. One thing, nevertheless, scared Femoo. There was an old man, clean -shaven head, rather stocky, that was forever weaving away at a basket on the only path that led to the stream. He wondered why he was always weaving, never looking up.

What kind of basket was he doing all the time? Each time Femoo accompanied any adult to the stream, he would feel a serious foreboding, fear and a forest of negative emotions stalking his child-like mind! He would even scream, spill away the water that he was carrying in his small basin and hug the adult nearest to him whenever this strange man looked up at Femoo.

He recalled one day, on the way to the village stream, he suddenly sited the weaver. Femoo flung the basin of water as one would a hot lead. He jumped off the road and headed for the main road again. He knocked down an old lady. The poor mama *ewu*, (grandma grey hair) popularly called so because of her all white hair. She fainted. It took a combined team of prayer warriors to revive the old lady. Such was the horror caused Femoo by the strange weaver.

"What on earth could this be?" He always wondered. He never got any answer to this worrying and harrowing question.

However, the answer or rather the answers screamed out one unusual day. This man indeed was a very dangerous person! He had been stealing other people's cocoa beans at night. This was an ungodly and sacrilegious crime. Indeed, it was practically an unpardonable sin against Femoo's society. He was caught. But in order to escape such a shame, he committed suicide: another unusual act in the village. It was this wicked man's corpse that was brought to the police barracks on Femoo's arrival at home from School, on a weekend that attracted his attention. Many days, the people say, are for the thief, but only one day for the owner.

So correctly, Femoo's childish mind had been deeper and had been prophetic, far above what any adult mind could have fathomed or foreseen. So the elders are correct, after all. Evidently, a small child's hand cannot reach for things hidden on the ceiling rack but the adult's hand cannot enter into the gourds, either.

Some strange things may not be explained. How did the primary four teacher decide to give Femoo and his mates, six lashes of cane each on 6/6/66, just for them to remember the day? Some eyes, palms and pants were wet, but Mr. Rishade boasted that he was a Higher Elementary teacher! But God is the greatest. Are all these things pointing to our nature, creed or race? Only the Holy One can judge right. Man or woman is an ugly feature while alive but after death they become as pretty as a portrait. That is a Yoruba proverb.

But what next, after this horrible treat? Let's see Femoo in a different world.

CHAPTER 5
Dinner on the farm

Holidays, hurray!

During the long holidays, Femoo would go to the Alapata farm with his siblings. He would enjoy those days thoroughly. Granny would never refuse him anything. All he had to do was ask! In fact, Femoo had once heard Granny declare that she believed that she was the real mother of Femoo, and that what his biological mum did was to loan out her womb to deliver him.

Whoao! That's it. Hes got the master key he needed.

 Sure, he must try this great joker offered him on a platter of gold.

One day, he heard a hawker crying her ware: *"ose ero ree o"*, meaning, "here comes popular soap". Femoo cried and threw tantrums for it. He wanted to taste it.

'But Femoo, my darling, you don't want to eat soap do you?' Grandma, *Iya mi,* asked, throwing up her arms in utter frustration.

'Yes, granny, I do. Please buy it for me. They say it's popular soap. I love it!'

'But are you sure?'

'Yes, grandma, very sure'

Finally, granny caved in. She bought one wrap. Femoo quickly unwrapped the mystery that was carefully tucked away in two dry cocoa leaves. He tasted the black piece. Of course, it was soapy. He spat it out. Goats, rams, rabbits, fowls were all bought for Femoo to raise. The last promise given him was a donkey!

Sunny was his cousin, rather smallish but older than he. His parent's hut was just overlooking that of granny. Unlike Femoo, Sunny was from a polygamous home, had lost his father and most importantly, could keep dogs. Oh, how Femoo loved to keep dogs, too! Finally, Sunny's bitch gave birth and how pretty those puppies looked!

Femoo told granny that he wanted to buy a puppy. It was his for the asking.

Generally grey, with a wide splash of black colour on its back, Femoo named his puppy 'baby'. It was a faithful dog, always close to its owner. Femoo took it home at Ife at the end of the holidays. One day, it followed Femoo's dad at his departure from home at dawn. It was unfortunately knocked down by a taxi cab at the motor park, just at the moment that he realized it had followed him, and was about to retrieve it.

In town, granny had bought him a cat. What a great excitement that was! It was his granny's way of getting rid of mice and rats then rampant in their new house, relatively isolated in the remotest part of Moore quarters, in the early 1960s. Femoo recalls, one day the cat had littered and was teaching its kittens hunting games. It had caught and brought home a life rat for the kitten to practice game hunting with.

The rat was trying to escape from its certain death so it jumped under the old sofa in the sitting room. Olu, his younger brother, who loved game meat with pounded yam, grabbed the wounded rat. The rat grabbed Olu with its incisors. With a bloody finger, Olu let go of the rat. Its intended owners resumed their sport under the old sofa.

On the following holidays, Femoo got another puppy and it was also named like the first dog. It didn't take long before the dog littered. Femoo had suddenly become a proud owner of eight dogs. All sorts were there:

the strong, the weak, the fair and the ugly. They were of different Colours too. Some resembled their mother while others had taken after their various fathers among the horde of male dogs milling round granny's hut. A special pen had been set up by granny in the kitchen for the puppies and their mother.

A hunting expedition for boys.
The cool breeze of after rain encouraged Ojo, the villagers' rascal to assemble his hunting party. Femoo was first on the line. He was brave enough and now was coming of age.

But also his grandma was a member of the elders council.

So one strange afternoon at the village Alapata, Femoo was alone. It was after the rain.

Ojo whistled. Baby was lying on the un-cemented but charcoal dyed floor. Femoo was feeling her very cold nose. The loyal hunting African dog corked her ears, stretched and yawned, lapping her black mouth with the long red tongues. She jumped out. Femoo followed. Soon, they were four. There was Mudashiru, quite frail, always begging for snacks. His half-brother, Laisi. plumb but could steal the day from God if he didn't pay attention.

Ojo led on, while the three boys filed behind him, with Baby bearing the rear after her master. The path was cold and grew colder as the foursome dug into the farm leaving behind the smoky homesteads. They opted for rat hunt. Ojo captained, so he decided where to go this time.
The plantain -cum -banana stem hunting was the easiest. A single boy could just with the left hand, squeeze up the top of the harvested and dry stem, and with the right hand, beat silly the stem downwards. He would then slit open the stem with a machete. There you could have up to seven rats unconscious or dead. If one was unlucky, some predator

36

snakes could charge out of the opened plantain stem. What to do then? Oh boy! Run for your dear life. Some boys had been beaten by snakes before.

Then, came the sharing time! Usually after about three hours of a hunting expedition, the boys would share the game. The eldest, or the bravest or even the boy on whose farm the largest catch was made, would be favoured with an extra rat or snail. However, Femoo would not be with them for long before he would hear granny calling him through the length and breadth of Alapata.

'You boys, Ojo bellowed, no messing around me, you hear?' Was just about thirteen but like an old gorilla, you won't teach him the forest path. He knew and could tell fresh footprints of game. He could tell which dropping was fresh or old.

'We'll try, *Oga* Ojo,sir! Muda whispered, fidgeting while Ojo fetched some four clubs from the thicket.

On return, he met the other three in a hot argument. Laisi said it was a snake hissing while the rest felt it was a cricket.

'That's a deadly snake hissing. You just don't move near, ok!'

Only Femoo, from town had a pair of rubber slippers called Dunlop. Each step swish- swish sound on wet leaves carpeting the palm and cocoa farm. Slippery it was, but Femoo relished this distinction for a town boy.

' sh... quiet, please! ' Ojo commanded, pointing to a stack of fresh palm leaves at the glade.

'*Oya! E de wayi o*! Come on, quick! Take position, now!' Baby jumped on the stack but Femoo restrained her. She growled.

The boys surrounded the stack.

Mudah started lifting the leaves by the broader end of the stalk. As the stalk reduced, Baby became more restless and whined. Two big rats ran in the same direction. Ojo

knocked down one and dropped it in his game bag. Mudah
ran after the other but slipped. Laisi tried to smash the
fleeing rat…but rather hit his brother by the heel. Blood
gushed out!

Femoo pursued but missed the brown hairy rodent. He was
giving up but Baby jumped and there the rat in her mouth.
Thumps up! She laid it at the feet of her master, wagging
her tail. He was very proud of granny's birthday gift.

They picked up some snails on their way home. The second
and third palm leaves raids had no rats living in them yet.
Ojo treated Mudah.

 They made it home.

Back Home

'Welcome, sir, chief hunter!' Femoo nearly answered.
 Grandma's sarcasm was obvious, with her short African
nose raised towards me.

She continued, 'And where are the antelopes or at least the
grass cutters, or no big game for us?'

The silence was broken by Laisi's screams and Muda's
shouts of *e gba mi o*, please save me! Their parents decided
to teach them lessons on how not to leave the house
without proper permission.

A misadventure

Femoo was battling with sleep on granny's mud bed. Akete
when Ojo's sonorous voice pierced his ears. He didn't like
what this village rascal had turned into ridiculous Yoruba
words the good Christian hymn. He sang a Capella,
beating his old hunting rods across his shoulders as Fulani
cowherds . His ringed fingers resounding

omitoro obuko, pelu iyan Koko

pada elese pada

Wa j'iyan koko

It was a famous repentance hymn he had bastardised
What Femoo had got used to at the CAC crusades was,

38

1. *E funpe na kikan,*
Ipe ihinrere
K' o dun jake jado
L' eti gbogbo eda;
Odun idasile ti de;
Pada elese, e pada.

The English version of Charles Wesley's hymn
Blow ye the trumpet, blow!
The gladly solemn sound
let all the nations know,
to earth's remotest bound:

The year of jubilee is come!
The year of jubilee is come!
Return, ye ransomed sinners, home

Granny snored. It was full moon and a few bats hovered around some thatched lonely kitchens that stood outside the main houses. Finally, Femoo devised a way to kill sleeplessness. He tiptoed and peeped through the only small window in her room.

Baby scratched the Dutch door outside the narrow sitting and largely multipurpose living space. She growled and as nobody responded, she led her puppies away to sleep. She came to the windows pot to acknowledge the half opened. As soon as she spotted the silhouette of Femoo, she wagged her tail and barked. Granny woke up.

Feeding the puppies was fun to Femoo. It was pap in a basin. At times, some coconut cream was added to the meal in order to protect the puppies from skin diseases. Some would overeat, while the runt was usually underfed. Calling them to eat was equally great fun. Of course it was an open call to all dogs. The call usually went like this: '*gbaa gbaa! Aja alaja gbaa gbaa*! This, more or less, means, 'come on, dogs belonging to various owners come along!' Femoo would pack his puppies into a basket, and then have to shoo away the rest.

After their meals, the puppies could indeed be playful. They would start by running one after another, with their tummies bulging on either side, probably learning game hunting. Then they would act some seriously fierce battles. Some would bare their snow white teeth, their claws and bark as loud as their puppy voices would allow. Dust was raised. They even divided themselves into teams and practiced what Femoo thought was a school relay race.

The puppies, with age, used various objects as targets of their hunting tricks. They could use stranded bones, handkerchiefs, granny's handbag or even babies' shoes or socks. They grew up gradually and upgraded their games to harassing older dogs passing in front of Femoo's hut. Baba Amada had about thirty-five dogs.

He was a hunter. Whenever he returned from his farm and hunting expeditions, the barking and inter group skirmishes of his horde of dogs would herald his passage. Of course Femoo's smaller pack would lay ambush on the larger groups, probably to assert that that area was theirs. Then Baba Amada would emerge, in his game blood tinted Khaki shorts and waistcoat, carrying his Dane gun across his shoulders resting his two muscular arms on the time-tested local gun.

Obi, an ingenious gunsmith from Awka, was very efficient in Alapata. He made and repaired guns. Children would take turns in pushing his bellows for him. Of course the aim was not to help him fan the flame of his kiln, but to enjoy the fun of seeing the fiery flame that palm kernel shells could produce. That was the limit for boys' adventure into Obi's domain. Nobody dared come near his anvil or lift his hammer. Those were sacred preserves of Obi and his first child!

Once Femoo's puppies were almost sold out, the remaining one or two fairly old dogs would turn guard dogs for granny's hut. Their feeding times coincided with those of the family. Not feeding them was impossible. The dogs, crouching around their master and other members of the family, would pester Femoo at every hand-to-mouth move. It was such an interesting show.

When he cut a morsel of food from the bowl, the dogs would accompany the move with their sharp eyes with their tongues dropping over their lower teeth. At times they would salivate too. On dipping it in the stew the dogs would trace their master 's fingers too. So the show would go on, usually at every dinner. If anybody attempted to place his or her meat on a plate on the floor, the smartest dog, naturally assuming it was meant for it, would snatch it.

The lucky dog would then rush to a safe distance to savour its meat. Any delay on its part could be dangerous as a horde of other stray dogs would have surrounded it trying to snatch the meat from the luckiest dog. As the dogs grew, feeding them became more difficult. This probably encouraged or pushed them to learn to fend for themselves by going hunting on nearby farms. The lazy ones pursued unsuspecting lizards and other harmless rodents. Such is life.

The mother dog, 'Baby,' would go hunting and bring home to Femoo big grass cutters. It was an unusual dog. It even had a puppy that was a hybrid. It was purchased at four shillings by the village night guard because it was male. Female puppies were one shilling dearer. The village night guard, a professional hunter, however, refused to pay Femoo. He tried to ask the guard to pay him his four shillings but granny warned him not to. Perhaps because the hunter had hard, or strong arms, a euphemism for being powerful in juju or charms. In the end, it was probably granny that paid for the puppy. It was shortly before the Nigerian civil war of 1967. Femoo bought a white shirt with the proceeds. The red-buttoned shirt served Femoo in the Church Choir. Daddy had argued that the proceeds of dog sale should not be taken to the Church. Some felt that was a Judaist view point and not Christian. But who could argue much before or against the 'Tisa'(the villagers' usual corrupt way of calling 'teacher') a retired British imperial police officer, well versed in Latin, Queen's English and rudimentary criminal laws?

Dinner on the farm, by the decree of granny, a great farmer, was usually as early as 5 pm. Mostly it was pounded yam or amala,

One could always understand why. Farming was tedious and strenuous, spanning the whole day. If Femoo had gone to the school football field to play, he would be fished out and hurried home to have his dinner warm. This was one of the great graces of staying with granny. Usually, because of the heat, dinner was taken outside on a well spread out mat. Moon light tales.

At the end of dinner, granny would tell stories. While granny sat on her raffia palm stool, the children crouched around her on the mat used to sun dry cocoa beans during the season. One of the children had the duty of holding the earthen palm oil lamp. The person holding it must also adjust the wick made of cotton lint soaked in palm oil, put in place with a triangle-shaped potsherd or china of similar shape.

Most of the times, the night stories, called alo in Yoruba, were about the old wily, wise tortoise, the husband of 'Yanibo', the beetle. The tortoise was always playing one prank or the other. Some of the stories have become so instructive that they are now wise sayings among people.

One of the tales that impressed Femoo most was the one in which the tortoise succeeded in making a king to eat the tortoise droppings. It runs thus: at a time of famine, the tortoise had boasted that the king could eat its droppings. Of course the royal father said such a thing was impossible.

The cunning animal asked the king what he would give him if he succeeded in making the royal father eat his droppings. The king promised to give tortoise a half of his kingdom, including his daughter.

However, not long after this wager, the tortoise, ever full of tricks, gave the king a package of honey-coated meal. Obviously the king wanted more of it and demanded to know where the tortoise got the delicious pack from.

- "From the thick virgin forest far away", the tortoise replied.

- "Quick, get me some!" replied the king. And off went the slow reptile. In the forest he would coat his droppings with honey or dates and packed them neatly to bring to the king.

At long last he reached the palace and delivered the special meals to the king who relished them and shared them with his family and chiefs. In the end, the king demanded where the tortoise got such special meals from. The animal disclosed that they were his droppings. The tortoise was not only given praises by the king he also got his wager: half of the kingdom and marrying the king's daughter.

"-What did the story teach us?" Granny would ask the children who eagerly swallowed every bit of her story and would want more. Usually granny would teach that children should be wise, as wisdom could promote them to wealth and raise their status as the tortoise in this story.

Femoo also loved the story of the monkey and his friend the tortoise.

How was the story of the tortoise and its friend the monkey? Granny told Femoo and his friends who had gathered in front of their hut as follows:

One day, the tortoise passed by the monkey's colony and offered a prayer: "May we never be punished for crimes that we never committed". However, the monkey never said amen. This silence of the monkey was considered as an insult by the tortoise. So he decided to punish the monkey. "He will pay dearly for not saying amen to my prayers", promised the tortoise.

How could he punish the monkey, a bigger, stronger and faster animal? The cunning tortoise therefore headed for the forest. There he made some sweet honey-coated meals which he offered to the king. Naturally the royal father asked where the tortoise got them.

- "Your majesty, long live!" greeted the sinister tortoise. They're the droppings of the monkey!" However, said the slow reptile, he would only discharge such a delicious meal if he is well beaten, especially on his belly" Having said this, the tortoise crawled away to his cave.

- "Quick, get me the monkey!" the king ordered. The king's messengers, who were kings of messengers, pounced on the monkey in his colony and dragged him to the palace. He was locked up in a dark room and politely asked to release those delicious droppings of his for his majesty. Puzzled, the monkey pleaded that he hadn't such mellow meals in his belly. He was whispering to deaf ears. His majesty, regarded as next to God, would not hear such rubbish. The relative of the chimpanzee and gorilla therefore, stretched out on the cold floor, and went to sleep. A few hours later, the messengers came in and looked round for the special meals but found none and they reported to the king.

-"Pound him very well on his stomach and you will have the sweet meals!" commanded the king. The messengers did so until the poor monkey fainted. There were various droppings but none was delicious. So the monkey was let off. He crawled away with his long tail hidden in his laps.

There was the tortoise near the monkey. The slow reptile asked his friend whether he would like to say "amen" now to the same prayer he had ignored. The monkey, still groaning under pains, yelled, 'amen!', 'amen!' and headed for the thick forest. Since then, granny concluded, the monkey had always jabbered 'amen!', 'amen!' everywhere!

This story teaches us to beware of bad friends and not to despise prayers however useless they may appear.

Another very interesting and educative tale is that of two women married to the same husband. The senior wife was wicked while the younger wife was kind. The younger wife was always maltreated and overworked. She had only one son. Soon the younger woman died, leaving behind her only son. The boy soon became a complete orphan as his father also passed on. His life was made miserable as his mother's senior partner literally enslaved him.

One day, he was sent to the farthest forest to clear a thick portion for planting. As he worked himself to the last drop of sweat, weeping and wailing over his misfortunes, an angel appeared to him. He offered the boy two beautiful balls and asked him to take them home. He was to go home and lock himself in and he was to smash the quiet ball and leave the noisy one alone. This the orphan boy did, behind closed door. There came out of the ball: food, toys, money, servants, etc. He became an instant billionaire.

His stepmother, full of jealousy, headed for the forest to also make a fortune. She equally met an angel who offered her two strange balls. She was instructed to go home, lock the door behind her and smash the quiet one to the floor.

She, however, thought the angel must have deceived her. So she instead smashed the noisy one to the floor of her locked room. Immediately came out snakes, other reptiles and dangerous animals that pursued her. She died for her wickedness.

What does the story teach? Wickedness does not pay, you must surely reap what you sowed, and God loves orphans and takes cares of them.

Granny also used to narrate some of her childhood experiences. She recounted how she and her members of her age grade groups would get a contract to carry baskets full of cocoa beans to Oshogbo railway station, about forty-five kilometers from Ife. They would return in the evening carrying other goods to sell at Ife and would still be strong enough to pound yam for their friend's wedding ceremony. She also told her grandson that she used to travel on foot to trade with the Ijaws who were riverine people. They could swim better than fishes of the seven seas, she boasted. She said there was highly profitable business there such as dried and fresh fishes and various sea foods to buy in the riparian land. The only danger, said she, was that of losing your wallet belt and risking getting drowned should you be discovered by the pirates, to have much money.

There was also the story of the friend of granny's dad who came in the night to sell his daddy for three pence. The poor mid -western tenant farmer came weeping and lamenting loudly about his father that had just died. He prostrated full length and begged great grandpa to please purchase his father for three pence if the old Ife man could whisk him off to roast quickly. What an odd proposal, you would shout, wouldn't you?

The riparian Middle Westerner, popularly called , Baba Isobo, had set a trap for game on his rented farm. However the trap caught an iguana! By his people's tradition, an iguana if killed by them must be given a burial befitting for a father. He must buy a nice coffin, slaughter a he-goat, and give wine to relatives. To avoid these expenses, he, a rather smart guy, was proposing to Femoo's grandpa to help purchase the reptile for three pence and simply roast it for dinner.

Grandpa, we were told, offered one penny as last price. He then threatened to report the case to the iguana seller's ethnic group. The poor man stopped haggling over his ancestor and quietly agreed. So Femoo's grandpa saved Baba Isobo …he roasted his ancestor for dinner. What a deal!

CHAPTER 6
What's up in Town?

Back in town after the holidays, Femoo rejoined his urban friends and play mates. Honestly, people would think life was very boring in town, as generally he walked in a triangular fashion. Was it, Home-School-Church? Oh no! There were by far more exciting side shows than met the eyes.

At school, now in middle class three, they had started to use nib-pens, ink wells inserted in the holes bored to the top of their desks. There was a girl, Yemi, who was notorious for drinking ink, ever sticking out her dyed tongue. Some new boys had joined the class. They were usually children or wards of police officers or some other government functionaries. Their parents were either produce inspectors or transferred teachers. The more indeed the merrier it was.

Variety is the spice of life? May be.

There was however, a friend closer to Femoo's heart: Kanbi. His father was a washerman and his mother sold eko, wrapped in leaves and carefully arranged in a big basket. His mother even supplied the food to secondary school hostels. She was so meticulous in the preparation of the corn or maize meal. She would soak the maize grains in big earthen pots for about three or four days, clean out the coats of the grains and ground them at the miller's. Then it would be sieved and the chaff sold to feed goats or other animals. The resulting *ogi* was partly sold for making pap or porridge. The rest was placed on a big earthen pot on heavy fire and stirred till it was done after about two to three hours. This is called 'eko' or 'ori' in Ife dialect.

Femoo had often been allowed to play at Kanbi's place within the mission complex of the Church before his friend's parent moved. They were so fond of each other in spite of the lowlier social status of the family of Kanbi. They even invented their own language called *"Ajuruna'*. As far as Femoo could recall, it was his friend that invented it to beat the class teacher's ban on vernacular, or Yoruba, speaking in classrooms.

The language code comprised adding some strange prefixes and suffixes to Yoruba language and varying the accents. The two boys were so fond of each other that parting after late talks became very difficult, if not impossible. They had to divide the distance between their homes into two equal parts and having seen each other off two or three times, without knowing when and where to part and bid each other the painful farewell, they would reach the agreed middle way and turn homewards.

Kanbi was a great calligrapher, while Femoo was described "as good as a hawk would write" at writing scripts, although he was the fastest in class. The two great friends, however, parted when his friend was discovered to have committed a serious offence at school. It was such a sad thing for Femoo. It was as if a hawk had snatched away a twin sister of a young fowl.

It was a joyous occasion for Femoo as he reached the sixth class of the elementary school and it was time to graduate. The rather shrewd headmaster, an Ijeshaman, Mr. Michael Oshun, an extremely brilliant grade one teacher an expert in Agriculture, had his last joker for all would-be graduands. Had he not taught the pupils deep agric science like nitrogen-fixing bacteria in nodules of groundnuts as azotobacter and nitrobacter?

He had, in 1967, taken the class to the new University of Ife to behold the breath-taking beauty of the campus which was constructed with their parents' cocoa revenue. The pupils had all vowed to study hard and not waste their parents' efforts. They must mould two thousand mud bricks for the extension of the school the following year.

The Parent and Teachers' Association had voluntarily contributed the sum of five shillings per pupil and Femoo's mum was the treasurer. They were divided into four groups of about eight boys each. The girls fetched water from the nearby stream. They later learnt that the place where the blocks were moulded was actually the newly built house of the HM's wife, herself a school teacher and mother of one of Femoo's classmates. His group under the captainship of Abiodun from Okene, faithfully completed its quota of five hundred blocks within two working weeks.

The oldest college in Ife, Ijesa and probably Ekiti land, Oduduwa College, founded in 1931, was nicknamed, 'Oducco Varsity'. It was one of the *Ionian colleges*. At the back of the boys' hostel were two fish ponds separated by a mound of laterite with overgrown grass that served as a short cut between Femoo's playground and the high school. The pond was fenced and the back door locked with a guard, Bassey, ever watching around.

However, once in a year, the fish ponds were emptied, and the fishes caught. Then, one of the ponds was opened to the public to fish in the muddy pool. One year, Femoo was the lucky one among his siblings. He caught a cat fish from the mud. As he could not drag it out, a cousin, Ade helped. Sharing the fish then became a problem.

High School at last!

Femoo had succeeded in the secondary school entrance examination. He would go to the beautiful Catholic School at the padre's hill, *Oke-Atan*, where the light shone at night. Really, St John's Catholic Grammar School was a show stopper any day. The Reverend Fabian had literally transplanted the Canadian model to Ile- Ife, the cradle of the Yoruba. Situated on the *Atan* hill, in the eastern part of the city, with a long driveway Boulevard, lined on either side by whispering pines, the school was really a city on a hill which Christ said could not be hidden.

The classrooms were large, with clean window-panes and huge lockers. They were storey buildings painted milk while the pillars wore ox blood. There were: a standard football pitch, practice fields, equipment for weight-lifting, huddles, and tennis and volley ball courts. There were even fish ponds and especially boreholes that supplied treated water for drinking, equally well equipped science laboratories for physics, chemistry, biology and agriculture. The admin storey building was the first after the drive in and housed the staff rooms, and the principal and the VP offices. The later was an accredited referee, from Ogbomoso, dark, svelte, spotting the typical ethnic marks, a graduate of history of the University of Ife, Mr. Anthony Alamo.

Granny finally disclosed that going to that school had been her dream for a very long time. Why that school? She had (seated each evening on the traditional petrol tank-turned-arm chair in front of her husband's compound at Ilode) watched in total admiration and was actually overwhelmed by the orderliness and the immaculate white shirts over khaki shorts, matched with sunlight bright tennis shoes of the Johnian boys! And she had vowed that her own son must join this happy throng, no matter how late in life.

Thus Femoo was not only following the normal course of the modern age, he was not only gliding or riding on the wings of time, he was fulfilling the desires of his granny, and the fervent prayers of his evangelical parents.

Time and tide wait for no man. School had started earlier than in the elementary school. On the first day, he had been shocked by Rev. Fr. Fabian, the school principal and the de facto proprietor, who did not hesitate to call him by his full names, Femoo Olusakin. How on earth this non-

Nigerian could not only identify him but also tell all his names! What could his secret be? Femoo must find that out and quick too.

The mystery was not long in coming. The wise principal knew the psychological impact of telling names at first meeting with the pupils. He had fixed their passport photographs to a note-book and had written their names under them. He had studied them and mastered the links. The Principal must be commended for such initiative and for bridging the racial divide. Little wonder then that his Religious Knowledge classes were practically the ones that boasted most pupil's attention.

It was a day school but preparatory classes were compulsory. After the two o'clock closing time, pupils had to stay for the prep classes from four pm till seven pm. The Johnians were therefore called the 'seven to seven' students. It paid them off as the Catholic school produced one of the best results in the country. Before the form five students passed out, banks would seek the Principal's help to recommend any final year student whom they would employ. Such was the confidence employers reposed in the products of the school!

Every junior student had a regular portion to weed and maintain throughout the term. It was not easy for Femoo but there was a divine help. One classmate of his, whose name preceded his and therefore his neighbor at the manual labour work, was a special case. He was about five years older and therefore more experienced.

The friend from *Ipetumodu*, Akin, had been a farm hand on daily wages for years. His palms were callous with machete use in dawn-to- dusk weeding tasks and cocoa farm spraying pump use. When he clapped those palms they sounded and resounded as two pieces of lifeless wood. He entertained his mates by placing live charcoal on his palm to prove that he was not their age mate. A teenager's arm's length portion was to him, like a pinch of snuff in the nostril of an old snuff addict. Akin would clear his portion in less than ten minutes. That was not the interesting story but the fact that he would always clear more than a half of Femoo's portion in the process.

One day, during the third term exams, Femoo and most of his classmates hesitated at clearing their portions so they were reported to the labour prefect. He brought the whole class to the portions and everyone had to stand by his portion. Of course, he would look at the portion and pronounce the student "guilty".

When the labour prefect got to Akin's well cleared portion, he smiled at him and declared: "obviously, not guilty". Akin looked around and blurted out: "everyone is guilty" and I, "not guilty", why? Is it because I'm from Ipetu?"

Akin dived to the Yoruba traditional posture of prostration for appeal, and begged aloud in Yoruba: "giliti, giliti, e dakun e ba emi naa se ki n gilitio!" meaning, "guilty, guilty, please help me do it and make me guilty also!"

However, one thing was a hitch to Femoo's educational quest: poverty! His parents were both teaching and barely eking out a living. Despite their cocoa plantations, the Nigeria of late 1960s was not so favourable to cocoa farmers in the South West. It was learnt that Sir Ladoke Akintola, the then Premier could have cut the price of cocoa beans to spite the Ife people. He had reportedly directed them to plant calabash creepers like the savannah farmers of Ogbomoso'. Was this true? They were reported to have supported Chief Obafemi Awolowo, his arch enemy.

Since his parents could not pay the £35 fees, the lowest of about twelve secondary schools in Ife, he was sent out of class along with some of the most brilliant mates like Adu ,Akanni, Isiaka, Saka,Sikiru, Steve,Tunde, Wande, etc... The Nigerian Rev Fr, Eru, would then pursue all reluctant pupils out of the compound in the Principal's Peugeot 403. It was such a sorry site.

Femoo would imagine what lessons were going on in the classrooms on his way home. He once recalled his mum taking him to his grandfather's at Timi Agbale compound, close to the Oba's palace. Climbing upstairs was an ordeal. But Femoo was proud to learn that his grandpa was the first person to put up a storey building in Ife and that the pioneer edifice lost stability because the reigning Oba had directed it be reduced in height so grandpa would not spy on the Oba's harem of wives! Had grandpa been alive, an assiduous trader from Badagry to Epe via Lagos, maybe he could have helped his grandson. But dad opted for salaries. Usually, on getting home Femoo would be told to go to Alapata, the famous farm where daddy was teaching, or rather where granny was farming.

He would have wondered whether his contractor uncle couldn't have helped. His uncle, neighbour to the Olusakins, had one day asked his children to listen to Femoo's song, one hot afternoon. Sure, things had been so hard, even food was hard at getting.
Usually, on returning from school at about 2 pm, the aroma of lunch would welcome him.
He undressed and put on his play clothes;a pair of second hand short called *okrika wake up,* and t-shirt. But that afternoon the kitchen was cold. But the grace of the Almighty was abundant in favour of those who dared look up in faith and not down. Femoo decided to see a promising future as his Pastor had preached the previous Sunday.

Standing by the walls of his uncle's uncompleted red brick bungalow, he had been echoing one high life classic of optimism. It ran thus:
Ipo ola dara o, ipo ola (the status of wealth is good, wealthy status)
Ipo yi wu mi lopolopo,mo si maa de be o (I like this status so much I must make it)

Mi o ko ko na mil'ow (I don't care if it costs me money)
Mi o ko ko na mi l'aso (I don't care if it costs me even clothes)
But I shall be an important personality (*Ma d'eni atata*)
I shall become wealthy. (ma d'eni olola)
I shall be the person sought after by the world (*Ma d'eni t'araye nfe)*
If any head is to be crowned in future, I shall be the one!
(*B'ori ba n j'oba l'ola o mo ti ma de be o)*

But was this uncle, though a prince, better off? Was his pit latrine not almost swallowing his aged mum, Iya, apparently a septuagenarian, the other day? He had to employ the services of users of carbide to blow off the overfilled toilet: an illegal and dangerous thing to do. So things were also bad for those up, as they were for the lowly. We thought it was a joke when his uncle came to borrow his dad's Rally bicycle. Daddy had even at a time reportedly ridden it to Ibadan, 54 miles away. A bicycle was a considerably big asset in those days.

Dad had tried. He would boil coco yams and fetch fresh vegetables from the backyard, picked palm nuts for oil. He equally had sweet potatoes. Fowls were raised.

Oh guinea fowls! More interesting, daddy had guinea fowls! How did he get to that? Daddy, in the rainy season, had bought from Hausa traders fresh guinea fowl eggs which he placed under his hens sitting on eggs, having replaced the house fowl's eggs.

The guinea fowls were hatched by the hens and soon the compound was filled with young guinea fowls. They grew rather fast and wild. Soon they refused roosting in the kitchen but preferred perching on nearby cocoa and kolanut trees near the police barracks boundary.

In those days of mid and late sixties, English football pool betting had become popular. Especially among the poor and unemployed who were hoping to strike it rich by this game of chance. There was at Moore road, just after the police barracks towards Ilesa bye pass, later changed to Fajuyi road, a football pool printing house.

The printing press established by an Ijebu man, who once made it rich close the gap through pool betting, had as employees, many young men. Egg-betting was an industry that grew from dad's guinea fowl eggs supply. Some of the young men working at the English football pool houses as printers and technicians were playing a fast one. One of their tricks at egg-betting was to crack a fresh egg, empty it and refill it with melted candle wax. Of course such treated egg would crack any egg! They were discovered!

The great joy about guinea fowls was that they laid so many eggs. Some sixty, some up to eighty! So eggs were plenty for eating and sale. In those days, the local fowls would only lay eggs seasonally and the Israeli agric or hybrid fowls that could lay daily were only at demonstration farms like Oyere. Those white fowls were the preserves of the rich or experts.

Driven out of school, having been given one shilling, Femoo would trek to Oroto Motor Park, about four miles from home. He would board the afternoon lorry and arrive about 4 or 5 pm if it was not raining. Daddy would never hesitate to ask his little son to please go to granny who was friendly with the Cooperative Society/Cocoa Marketing Board loans facilities.

As if to witness the ritual of loan application, Femoo would then be taken by granny to the Cooperative Store, a rather imposing cement block-building with an extensive concrete, well fenced frontage for drying cocoa beans. Inside were jute or sisal bags of cocoa beans stacked in pyramids according to their grades. At the corridor were giant scales for weighing the bags and small tables and matching wooden chairs for the produce inspectors.

It was indeed a place of awe and salvation, at least for young Femoo who was by now praying fervently that the almighty Secretary of the Cooperative Society would grant the loan or the pesticides. If cartons of pesticides were granted out of season, granny would then sell them to richer farmers at about a quarter of the going price just for Femoo's fees to be paid.

First Trip to Lagos

His elder brother invited him to Lagos, 'Eko Akete, Ilu Ogbon', the City of wisdom as the Yorubas call it. After a Prize-winning result at school, he was rewarded with a novel titled Fire on the Mountain by John and Allison Tedman. His trophy was promptly rushed to his father at Alapata. His daddy had received the award, carefully wrapped with the principal's cursive etching out the surname. Sweat dropping off his brow, daddy muttered some words.

What was he saying? What could this soliloquy mean? This monologue could it tantamount to regrets? Probably he was thanking God for promoting this name among the whites again, decades after his exploits in the imperial police force. Or was he scrutinizing a successor after his departure to the great beyond? Only God probably knows.

His leather box, popularly called portmanteau, was well stuffed with edible items for his brother in Lagos. His cousin Lolu took him to the Lagere N. K. Zard cocoa store. The Zard brothers were believed to be Lebanese who came to Nigeria during or after the Second World War and were well entrenched in the commercial life of Nigeria. Interestingly, the Yoruba still call them 'Koraas', especially in Ibadan. Well, riding in the back space of a trailer heavily laden with tons of cocoa bean bags was the cheapest way of getting to Lagos from Ife.

In the back space, the body smell of the apprentice driver wafted with the aroma of the dry cocoa beans and made a great recipe for   nausea. When in the middle of the long and tortuous 200-mile journey, Femoo was moved to the front seat, the engine heat was becoming a miniature hell compartment for the village boy.

Femoo notice that aeroplanes were rather flying low, and there were more cars on the road. Unlike back home, no boys were waving at the planes and shouting at them prayers for foreign cakes and good luck. May be because it was late? But then, what about this snake-like lines of vehicles on the road? He finally gave voice to his curiosity:

-*"Buoda, S'a a ti d' Eko?"* "Brother, have we arrived in Lagos"?

- "Not yet, this is Ikorodu", came the short reply. It was about 7. 30 pm. They had set out at about 2. 30 pm, this is aside from almost one hour at the cocoa store, waiting for the best trailer. They finally got down at Maryland, crossing the heavy traffic jam, for which Lagos was famous. They shortcut through the Palm Grove Estate, each carrying his load. Femoo was showed, by his cousin, the Shonibare Estate and various investment landmarks built by past Western Regional leaders. Finally, they emerged in Mushin, his Uncle's place.

Soft boiled black-eyed beans with fresh bread was the staple food in Lagos. It was truly a life of "*b'ooji, o ji mi*", that is, Yoruba for; "If you wake please wake me up too" They would wake as early as 4 am, not for early morning prayer meetings as at Ife, but in order to beat the bathroom queue and the unending traffic jams *of Musin, Alakara, Atewolara, Aswani, Oju Elegba, Osodi.* Or there could be the Costain constraint or traffic bottleneck at 7 Up.

His brother had secured a space for Femoo in Baba Bola's room, on the ground floor of the storey building at No 9 Tinuoye Street, Olorunsogo. The svelte, dark-skinned, middle-aged Egba tenant, who had a white vespa scooter, then a high school teacher, gave the space free (most of the young men were struggling to pass the Advanced Level GCE examinations. They wanted to gain admission into any of the five Nigerian main universities of: Ibadan, Ife, Lagos, Zaria, and Nsukka).

Femoo's place for the night rest was a sufficient mat space between the veneered record changer cum radio set and his benefactor's spring-mattress bed. It was such a completely different world from Femoo's cock crow/church bell announced dawns at Ife. Here, it was the juju music of Chief Ebenezer Obey's miliki band records that would wake Femoo up, with either his highly philosophical or spiritual Ketekete or the Donkey Saga or King Sunny Ade's eulogies of the gods laced with highly scintillating guitar display.

There were many of his uncles and nephews all over the city. What! In Lagos Femoo also saw people making money from clearing septic tanks. Visits were organized to: Race Course, with the nearby 25-storey Independence Building, the Bar Beach, and popular name of the Lagos beach. He could also visit the Ikeja Airport, etc.

He was able to use the escalator at the Kingsway stores and had chocolate bars at the Leventis store located close to each other on Broad Street by the marina. He even looked out for dolls that he was told could speak like human beings and rush promptly to the door, reeling out their inventory of goods for sale, as soon as one stepped into the Kingsway stores.

The airport was exciting. His engineer uncle, Legan, showed Femoo into one of the small fixed wing aircraft. That was the ultimate!

He even started visiting by himself on the red-white-red Lagos City Municipal Transport Service (LMTS) buses. Usually overweight, khaki-uniformed male/female bus conductors with heavy ticket machines on their chests, stylishly winding them, as they collected the two to three pence per drop bus fares and fished out crafty passengers who rode for free. One or two times a week, Femoo missed his bus stops either on his way to Sangross or Ikeja. Not much damage done, as people were always ready to help the upland boy, should he be completely confused.

One Sunday morning, he saw a fatal accident scene. An overturned Kombi bus with victims, Bibles, lying side by side, in their pool of blood! Lagosians just passed by as if nothing had happened. Femoo stood transfixed. How would he move with human lives lost? His brother beckoned him to move on as a Lagosian.

Also, even his people in Lagos seemed to have lost most of the typical Nigerian hospitality. One Sunday evening, his British-trained uncle had invited him home in Surulere. His brother, having lived in Lagos longer and wiser, had warned Femoo to have lunch before visiting his uncle. He didn't think that was good manners. When he got there, his uncle's foreign wife warmly received him. He was served a grilled sole fish as thin as a sheet of paper.

All he had it with was a small bottle of criminally cold Guinness stout. He had never been offered such before, but at least he had been recognized as growing up too. Pangs of hunger twisted and turned Femoo's tiny tummy and he aborted the visit and rushed home.

The lessons had been slow at coming. Femoo didn't want to be hasty and assume wrongly. He had learnt: our people, once in Lagos, lagged in lasting hospitality, were lower in patience, lean in love, and often lividly lash at slow and lowly visitors.

He would have to review his interest in staying and living this kind of life. Second-hand jeans shorts, long-sleeved Elvis Presley shirts, and a few items for siblings and people at Ile-Ife, the cradle of all, were bought for him at the famous Quay side, Marina. Femoo returned home with glee.

He returned to school, and when fine arts were introduced, Femoo was quite skillful, especially in painting. He still recalled vividly how his year three class decorated the newly completed dining hall. Oh, talk of the dinning hall and the memories of the school prefect who loved high-sounding words but was rather poor in English will rush on! He had to be made prefect probably because he was catholic as all prefects had to be. He spoke of massacring younger pupils' rations. He would not hesitate to inject names of weeds like 'calopogonium' and 'centrosema', if only to impress the younger and gullible pupils that he was quite hot upstairs.

The rest, like Femoo, however competent they were, could only be presidents of clubs or strictly academic groups such as the literary club, the French club etc…etc. Femoo was somehow distraught but his older siblings reminded him that the Catholics owned their school and some of them had to be given some sense of belonging.

Naturally, having stayed long with granny and attended elders' council, Femoo was very good in Yoruba proverbs and idiomatic expressions. So when it was time to choose subjects in form three, he opted for Yoruba, instead of French. The principal politely but with convincing reasons reoriented him to choose French, a language that would hold more hope in future. Moreover, the head teacher assured Femoo that he could score higher marks in French in his West African School Certificate Examinations than in Yoruba. It turned out to be exactly so. The principal was prophetic.

CHAPTER 7
Too Armed to Judge Here!

Femoo was back in the village again during the long vacation. It was always a great joy to break away from the usually tense family routine in town. He had been looking out for tell-tale signs of changes in the village once the old *bolekaja* was approaching the village, Alapata.

One couldn't mistake it. What an impressive site! The fierce anger of the main river that lashed the land of their neighbours, splitting woods and spitting and splattering rubble, entered Femoo's village totally pacified. This river merely simmering, soothing as it whispered and wove its tortuous way over rocky parts and mounds under oil and raffia palms, flanked by green and luxuriant canopy of stately hard wood trees, was all theirs here.

Femoo could now understand while white geese and ducks and ducklings floated majestically all day over this peaceful river. What a scene! Mother duck floating followed by an Indian file of about twenty-two ducklings. They were so orderly. He could still remember splashing water at his siblings and mates whenever granny came to fetch special *Gbago* leaves to protect and preserve her kolanuts. She was a kolanut merchant of some means.

These had stood as brave sentinels over the years at the entrance of their village. So the rocky beds and banks of the river gave the village its name, Alapata, meaning the rocky place. Would you blame his ancestors for giving in to this captivating site? So they settled to drink in full the cups of beauty that nature had set before them in such a generous quantity and quality.

Respect for elders was effected to the letters among Femoos' people. Any sign of disrespect or deviance was severely punished. That was typical of the Yoruba. One evening, granny had sent Femoo to pick up some 'esusu', or cooperative contribution from one of his uncles popularly called, "uncle Lemuel, ajeku ekun". Femoo promptly left for the uncle's hut at the upper stream part of the village. He located the hut of his stocky, pot-bellied uncle. He asked for uncle '*Lemuel, ajeku ekun*'.

-"Did you say that or it dropped from your foul mouth?" the first but elderly child charged at Femoo. That was the first warning shot.

-"Brother, please don't beat me up, that is the uncle's name, isn't it?" Femoo asked with all the aura of innocence wreathed around his childish voice.

Out of excessive anger, the teenager missed his target, and drove his punch into the grilling metal basket suspended over the heath. Decades of soot baptized both the victim and his tormentor. Femoo, escaping as a scared chick from the claws of a careless eagle, ran for his dear life. He was soon in his granny's hut. Panting, he asked why the appellation uncle Lemuel the tiger's leftovers, was causing such a stir among his children.

Granny now explained that while the uncle was a baby his mother left him crawling outside while she stepped in to pick something in the hut. Before she could return his baby had been picked up by a tiger. Raising an alarm, hunters raced to her rescue, spoke some spiritual words to the tiger which vomited the baby. The baby had survived, but the tiger had probably destroyed one of the baby's thigh nerves tendons or even the ham. Hence the uncle now limps on one leg.

It was in the dangerous days in Nigeria. The leader of the Action Group party was seeking alliance and political thuggery was beginning to manifest openly in the south west from Femoo's reckoning.

There was palpable tension written all over the city. Dangers were all over the place. Not only were the guards not at ease, even, the elders were worried. Parents had clearly warned their children and wards to watch out. As dad told Femoo "not only is there grave danger at Longe's farm, even Longe himself is dangerous", in Yoruba.

The elders' council usually held in front of the village chief's hut. It was an open place surrounded by huts of Sunny's parents, that of Femoo's granny and another of the senior female partner of Granny's. Usually, non-members wouldn't move near it. It was the rule of the thumb: members knew one another. They were the rulers of the village that advised the Baale, the chief. It is believed he could also co-opt anybody that he felt would be relevant to their discussions or rather debates. However, such special members would only attend specific meetings unlike permanent members.

How did it happen that Femoo should be at the elders' council that night? Certainly, a lad like him would have no advice to give the elders. After all, his people always say "no matter how hard things may turn for a father on earth, he will never appeal for help from his son who had died before him". Was granny interested in seeing his face? Were these elders also interested in keeping company of a youth?

They had been meeting for three days with no decision taken on the only issue brought before them. Granny had been a member of the village council in her capacity as one of the most senior women leaders and foremost Christian leader. She was equally famous among the poor foreigners in the village. She was their saviour, freely helping to deliver their pregnant women of their babies wherever the labour set in. Femoo had been carrying her granny's hurricane lamp so he could follow the elders' debates. He would battle with the heat and smoke from the kerosene lamp as well as the moths flying around the yellow flame shade.

Once in a while shrills of bats would sift through the thick forest of the elders' thought. As some of the elders dozed off, a couple of bats, probably attempting to mate, would bank overhead, and vanish into a few thatched roofs, relics of the reluctant abject poverty stalking the villagers. If a meteor flew past, with twigs of lights, the elders would smack their lips several times so these wizards wouldn't strike them. So Femoo learnt.

"-What a terrible thing now in our midst! But how far will things have to go before we arrest them?" one of the elders queried aloud.

-"Why bring such arms and ammunition to our village? Would somebody please shake off this nightmare from my mind!" wondered the other leader.

-"But it is impossible to ever think out such an evil plan even among our evil neighbouring villages!" the PRO asserted with an air of finality, his clean shaven head reflecting the surrounding lights.

-"My Bible teaches me that in the last days terrible things will happen. I hope the last days are not yet here?" "Femoo's granny thought.

For three nights now the elders of Alapata village had been trying to unravel this mysterious situation on their laps. Almost all of them confessed that such a knotty case had never been given their ancestors before. Some had prayed, in churches and in the only Jumat mosque in the village. Even chief Ali, who was also a traditional religion practitioner, disclosed that Ifa, the god of divination among the Yoruba, had been silent on this enigmatic matter.

Granny had equally been suddenly summoned to the compound of Chief Odu in the early hours of the day. Femoo could recall it was one of those nights, after a heavy downpour and sleep was very sweet, when granny rushed back to pick two swaddling clothes. It was later in the evening that he could fully understand what the clothes were meant for. They were to handcuff the suspects.

At the elders' council, Femoo had learnt that during the previous night two men had been caught by the village night guards. They had had to be detained in one of the

Chief's inner rooms. They were caught as thieves. But what was unusual and shocking about them was the type of arms they were carrying to do their wicked act!

While Femoo was busy battling with the main assignment that brought him there, carrying granny's hurricane lamp, the exhibits, instruments of terror, were laid out. First were the heavy ropes to tie up would-be victims. Then one heavy electric torch: to blind whoever dared to look at them. Equally, there was on the floor a double edged machete to hack any challenger. There was also a catapult! A dangerous set of weapons indeed! They had also abandoned at the entrance of the village a wooden ladder to climb into people's homes.

After much serious debate by all the members Femoo' dad was given the floor in his capacity as an ex-policeman, full of British laws. He said many things but the long and short of it was that the thieves were too armed to be judged in the village elders' court. He felt that the peace they came to disturb belonged to the Federal Government whose nearest agent were based at Ile-Ife. He even dared to accuse the elders of flouting the law by doing what he termed unlawful detention of free citizens without having a document he called a warrant of arrest. That was like pouring petrol into the flame of the elders' passion. Free citizens or what? The village chief lamented that elders had lost their powers. He disclosed that were it in the days of his ancestors, even his predecessors, he would have single-handedly dispensed the justice and disposed of these criminals.

The following day, the two thieves, eyes blood-shot, in now stinking black clothes were escorted to the town police station. They would face the Federal Government court or wrath. Well, the people say that any baby that will not let his mother sleep he himself will not know sleep. Their case is now like that of the proverbial bird that alights on an unstable rope. Neither the bird nor the rope will rest.

Even God says whoever breaks the hedge, the snake will bite him.

Will the legal snake ever bite them deep or even bite them at all? Will the loophole be widened to admit them? The elders and young Femoo wondered aloud: who will now serve them or the law?

CHAPTER 8

The. Charge Office
'Trouble! War!' *E gba wa o!* Please save us!
The shout of pandemonium rang through the Moore district police station.
It shattered the usual traditional calm and peace of the fearsome agents and only known face of the government at Ife of the mid-1960s.
The charge office is located at the center of the C-shaped police barracks. It's just at the edge of the clean whitewashed stones demarcating the large driveway. The field, usually overgrown, had seized cars, mostly accidented disorderly parked behind it. Some, grounded for ages, have their engine jutting out like the tongue of a crushed toad.
The breezy cold but dry harmattan lashed at any person or object standing on its erratic path.
The alarm raised in the early evening of breezy February hesitant harmattan, had dragged into the charge office a forest of legs.
Femoo peeping from his barrack boy's post could see them. Some were hairy, smooth multi gender, sweaty and some dry. There were heavy calves, as mortars, some tiny tots also sticking to the skirts of their milk givers. Everyone wanted to catch a glimpse of the latest scenario. The police barrack, or rather, the charge office was the only exciting cinema hall in the district. Politicians, their thugs and opposition groups are usually clamped into detention.
The inspector had just charged the sergeant with his three blood-red strips delicately bordered in black thread.
'sergeant match those criminals here, right now!'
'For interrogation sir or for...?' The corporal jabbing his index finger downwards, was interrupted. He won't let this fellow disclose what else they do there.

'Or for marriage ceremony in your village? And if you're not careful, you may lose one stripe before you celebrate a month of your promotion. You hear me?' Thundered the inspector.

He wiped his face, then he stroked down his two stripes as if to ensure they are not yanked off yet. He smiled.

The inspector coughed and sneezed covering his sweaty face with a dirty handkerchief, with blue and grey borders.

Corporal Abila stroked his tribal marks from his side temple to his chin, then raised his nose at inspector Nnamuku.

A dusty Agama lizard, with his orange and deep blue head rushed in but stopped short at the slightly raised doorway. It nodded three times. The corporal saluted him. The reptile rushed forward and headed for the paneled desk with dirty and tattered plywood. Candle wax flow had spread all over the desk as if to fill up the peeled plywood.

'Corporal, are you okay, saluting a lizard?'

Sargent Ojorokpor shook his head, and yawned aloud tried to backhand his gaping mouth but failed. He sneezed, and spluttered. 'Sorry, sir' to his superior.

The inspector, in no mood for jokes, stammered, 'you should feel sorry for yourself will you march the accused here forthwith?'

Then, a large iguana, probably disturbed by the released vehicle just towed away from the field, crawled into the office. Was it pursuing the lizard? It was most probably.

'My father! My father!' the accused shouted, caressing the bigger reptile.

'Your father, the iguana?' The inspector asked doffing his cap.

'*Una see, even Oga inspector dey salute* my father o!'

'And who is saluting your daddy? Me, a scaly iguana?' I just raised my cap for fresh air for my head o. But why are these fellows not fully handcuffed?'

'Sorry sir, it's not me o! It's the corporal'

Mouth agape, *emi ke?*. Me, God forbid bad thing o! Seargeant is in command, sir. I only obeyed him o.'
The crowd chorused, 'sir, *won ti gb'owo!'* They have been bribed.
Finally, the two accused fellows were marched before inspector Nnamuku.
But what's happening here? Femoo wondered aloud.
A cobra! Here it came in hot pursuit. It's black and grey rings in clear contrast with the brown tattered terrazzo floor. The king stood, staring the inspector on the face, it's hood stood intimidating.
Father of pandemonium!
  A cobra? It was first a lizard, almost harmless, then an iguana. Finally, to complete the trinity, a king cobra on a broad day light!
The cobra headed straight for the forest of feet. Father of pandemonium!
A scream from a boy in the crowd. Then an elderly woman yelled, *mo gbe o! O ti bu mi je o! I'm in trouble It has bitten me o!* By this time, everybody had scampered and the ring leader had escaped too.
When the dust settled the inspector, stood at attention.
'But wait a minute, sergeant!'
'Yes sir!'
'Quick, do a head count'
'Sir, we have as SOP directs sir. Only one person is missing... eh...eh, the new accused man from Alapata sir...the ring leader. But his accomplice is still here'
'And where did you leave him?'
'I don't know sir'
Soon, the corporal collared him at Bobor's, the sergeant's daughter's smoking joint.
He was dragged to the charge office.
He came in hailing the inspector, calling him all sorts of names.
'Go lock the stupid thing in the guardroom for me, alright?'

As they locked up Dudopa, alias red devil, there was a small wrap at the door of the guardroom.

'And what is that?'

Then came in Kayus, alias thunder Balogun, the captain of the Barrack boys football club. He was panting, clutching the leather football.

He spluttered, pointing at the wrap 'sir, that's from Bobor, the sergeant's daughter.

'Red devil was at the joint, sir. He was drinking and smoking while the snakes escaped from the car park.'

'Tell me, boy thunder, we're there many snakes?' The inspector asked.

'Sir, many snakes, sir. Even Jidex, your boy knows how to raid their nests in the cars. I mean, our football maestro, boy Jidex'

The inspector folded his hands and goggled at the bow legged boy. He opened his mouth so wide it could have swallowed a tennis ball.

He made straight for the wrap, gloved his hand and picked it up.

He screamed, 'Oh my God, this is *Igbo, cannabis sativa,* original marijuana! Did you say from Bobor's joint? Sergeant, what is this? And where is your Bobor in all these?'

'Sure, sir, Kayus reconfirmed. Or you want me to take you there, sir? But you know the place, now. *Se bi e mo now. Abi e fe gbe mi l'enu jo ni?* Of course, you know sir, or you just egging me on?

'Me?' Asked the inspector, shrugging. Both the sergeant and the corporal looked askance.

Boy thunder continued, 'they lace their beans with it, they use it to flavor their Okro stew and almost all other soup, pepper soup, goat meat etc'

'Sir, once they are high on this their special meal, they are possessed. They can go to war on any flimsy excuse.'

As boy Kayus exited., cries of *ogun o, iku ree, war!death is here rent the air.*

The boy was already having seizure while the elderly woman victim was already foaming in the mouth, King cobra has done its worse here.

CHAPTER 9
The Civil War Days

The boys were playing football at the frontage of Baba Pastor's house. It had been a very tough match. The football was a big cow bladder extracted from a slaughtered cow by Iwo butchers that abounded in Ile-Ife. Only God knows where granny learnt how to use the cow bladder as football. Perhaps from the highly enterprising butchers at the abattoir located at the Odo Eran area of town.

Femoo and his mates were engrossed in the dribbles and dodges of good players, when shouts of "E gba mi o!" Please save me! shattered the serenity of the air. There was the corpulent, ever- flamboyant Mama Barbara running at the topmost speed of an Olympic medalist.

Her colourful head gear, bangles, earrings, and gold-rimmed vanity case had all flown off and her sash gone with the wind but all these never stopped her a bit. She dashed into the senior pastor's house upstairs. The boys were tongue-tied. What demons could have pursued one of the most powerful politicians like her?

The boys had picked the various items that fell off the wealthy lady and had rushed to return them to her. However, she was nowhere to be found upstairs in the visitors' sitting room. Where could mama have been? It was not long when another shouts of "come down! Push her down!" reached them from downstairs.

There were at the frontage four fierce-looking stocky men, torso exposed, full of muscles, covered with beads of sweat. They were puffing like angry adders, threatening to set the house ablaze if Mama Barbara was not released to them immediately. The ministers of God downstairs must have drawn their attention to the gaffe that they had just committed.

This is the house of the anointed of God. No matter how mad a dog is, it should at least still recognize its owner. The raging bull of political madness in the nation must not be allowed to tarnish the spiritual garment of the anointed ministers who still stand and serve faithfully at the altar of the Almighty God.

The foursome flexed their heavy biceps and chanted some war-like songs people claimed to be in Bariba language (spoken in neighbouring Benin Republic and some part of Kwara State of Nigeria). They scratched frontage concrete with their double-edged machetes and sparks of fire flew off the ground in several directions. They equally belched out some foul and unprintable words, raising their short noses in the direction of Mama Barbara, upstairs. The old lady had sought and obtained full protection in the shadow of the Almighty.

As they jumped the gutter into the main street they swore to deposit Mama Barbara's head before sunset the following day. That was the sentence pronounced on her by Chief Petrus, the warlord of Action Group in Ife. The ever productive tropical palm tree was the party symbol. According to him, Mama Barbara had made the mistake of joining S. L. Akintola's evil party that chose the left palm as its symbol; the "Demo".

He had the wherewithal and all the instruments of terror at his beck and call. At the mention of his name cold shivers ran down spines of even valiant men. His district was a no go for those who claimed to be strong even in the United People's Grand Alliance, UPGA.

One evening, while mum was cooking, daddy suddenly scampered back home dragging a quarter-full jute cocoa bag with him. He related how he had witnessed some thugs tie hand and foot his buying agent, chief Bamise. In spite of various pleas and offers, they dumped him into his lorry full of grade -A cocoa bags.

They doused him with petrol and set him ablaze. Daddy shook his head in disbelief. Looking utterly dejected, he concluded the story of the Black man's shame, that the rich cocoa licensed buying agent cracked as cocoa beans and shrank releasing the smell of fresh flesh, grilled by evil men of politics greedy of evil.

The politicians were so reckless. One day at the blacksmith quarters called 'Ogbon Ido', the Land Rover jeep of NNDP, the Democratic Party, with loud speakers blaring slogans and a toddler shouted 'Awo ooo!' What? Was that not the name of the jailed AG leader?

The Demo thugs, amulets round their upper arms, jumped down and traced the shout into the room of the 85-year-old Baba Jimoh where his last grandchild, Yekinni, then under his paternal care, was warming himself in the early morning December Harmattan cold. They dragged out the poor partially blind octogenarian in his dirty, tattered, smoke-drenched danshiki garment. Then they beat him as you would a punch bag. He was left for dead about five miles away at the Ilesa bye pass road. Such was politics of wild western Nigeria.

Femoo's richer uncle whose trailer used to ply Kano had had to abandon the transport business because the roads were not safe any longer for non-Hausa speakers. The lorry was acquired on hire purchase terms! That was the beginning of his uncle's financial fiasco. A bailiff had come to 'five-a'his house! This actually means that the court injunction was taking possession of his uncle's house. The bailiff came in and sealed off the doors with wax! His house had been sealed off with a wax as a result of insolvency.

Finally, the politicians had climbed the proverbial tree beyond the leaves end and their drum pitch had been raised too high. Their drum had to break.

Yes, their drum did break. One day, Femoo heard a strange announcement over his mother's wooden radio box. It was a rediffusion box of Radio Nigeria, Ibadan. God be thanked that the two shillings and six pence monthly subscription fees had been paid and the short 1 inch by 3 cardboard-like receipts promptly stuck to the loud speaker's grill. The announcement came solemn but clear.

The male news caster declared: "In the early hours of today, some dissident soldiers abducted the Premier of Western Region, Sir Samuel Ladoke Akintola. The whereabouts of the deputy premier, Chief Remi Fani-Kayode are equally still unknown. We advise all citizens to go about their lawful duties.

Later in school Femoo was required to learn the names of the new leaders of Nigeria. The four Regions had new governors as follows:

-Col. Adekunle Fajuyi, an Ekiti Yoruba man, for western region
-Col. Chukwuemeka Odumegwu Ojukwu, an Ibo, for Eastern region
-Col. Hassan Usman Katsina, Hausa, Northern region;
Col. David Ejoor a mid westerner, for Mid Western region.

Later, Femoo also learn that in Lagos, the new leader was no longer the Hausa Prime Minister Abubakar Tafawa Balewa, but an Ibo, Brig. Thomas Aguyi Ironsi.

A few months later, again, one northern Hausa-speaking from the Middle belt, called Brig Yakubu Gowon, had replaced him. Two elders argued that the Ibos killed the premiers and leaders of the west, mid west, and the north but let theirs escape. The man was not done he even labeled them "I before others" the other elder retorted that the north Hausa/Fulanis were uneducated and lazy, always wanting government largesse. He dismissed the Yorubas as opportunistic and crafty.

Just one day, Femoo discovered that cars, Lorries, trailers were all over Ile-Ife town: the Ibos were returning home. Mum regretted losing her Christian prayer partners to recent unusual developments in the North. Shops owned by Ibos like the Maluo shops were closed down, and various items put on clear and sale.

It was learnt that Obi, an Ibo man, the best blacksmith, in Alapata, from Awka was molested. He was said to have been brought there since he was a toddler and spoke Yoruba like everyone else. His children, Emeka, Uche were all Femoo's playmates in Alapata. However he was rescued and sought refuge at the mission house where he was then living. What exactly was taking over the peaceful cities and turning Nigerians against one another only God could tell, Night vigils were organized at the CAC parishes.

One Sunday morning service there was a deep prophecy talking of a strange giant machine installed in Nigeria. Young men were offering themselves to it some were pushed to it and the machine kept swallowing the youths, mangling them and spitting out their blood.

The prophet wailed and moaned that the blood was flowing more in the East and gushed westwards till it stopped at a place called Ore. (at the eastern fringes of

South west Nigeria, in the present Ondo State) The elders of the Church set up a 24 hour prayer chain to decree that the blood flow should never pass Ore. Were they being selfish or self-preserving? God knows.

Civil war had started! Streetlights were switched off; daddy covered all fanlights to prevent the bombers of Col. Odumegwu Ojukwu, leader of the rebels, from recognizing the city of Ile-Ife. Femoo had been stampeded one day. Soldiers in camouflage fatigues had taken over the barracks field. They were recruiting strong and hefty boys. Guns had come. Granny had asked all teenage girls or pretty girls to hide away. She recounted how during Hitler war, in the 1940s, soldiers raped and raged all over the cities like hell let loose. She recalled that many girls were pregnant and gave birth to babies who would never know their fathers: a grievous curse on the land.

At long last, even in their school, recruiting officers had come. Femoo's classmate had joined the army. He was a pastor's kid. He came back maimed. Femoo's distant cousin, and Church member, was rejected because although thickset, was too short, rushed after the military land rover jeep of the recruiting officer and jumped inside it. Femoo watched the soldiers hugging him and probably congratulating him for being valiant. Brother Ola had pressed into it as into God's kingdom. He never returned. He was a promising fashion designer at Ile-Ife.

His mother prayed, fasted and ran from one prayer house to the other. Ridiculous stories were told her about her son. There were cock and bull stories of hearing his voice that he drowned at Onitsha sector. To keep Nigeria one, is a task that must be done, indeed! So the radio blared daily.

Femoo watched boys boasting about the feats of Nigerian war heroes. Some were praised by I. K. Dairo the famous juju musician. Some of them were like the black scorpion, Benjamen Adekunle, and his own near kin's man,

76

for whom the CAC fasted days, Col. Alani Akinrinade. There were Gen. Shuwa etc. Now guns, machine guns, sub machine guns, Kalashnikovs, and various pistols could be seen displayed by recruitment officers. Aside from his dad's Dane gun, and his friends' dad, police corporals who had double barreled guns, guns and weapons of war were not common in Ile-Ife in those days.

War was equally frustrating. The Biafrans made full use of propaganda. Femoo could recall one afternoon while playing football at the barrack pitch; he heard the voice of Biafra. It must have been Christopher Okoko Ndem. In his deep baritone voice, he stated clearly that the vandals of Yakubu Gowon were now surrendering en masse at the palace of the Ooni of Ife, Sir Adesoji Aderemi. He vowed that the rising sun troops of Biafra were going to have their breakfast the following day at the Dodan Barracks, Lagos, and the seat of Gen. Gowon's Federal Government.

Femoo was scared to death. He jumped, ran, skipped and screamed home. Panting, he related to his mother that the Biafran troops were already at the Ooni's palace. Mum threatened to hit Femoo with the ladle hot with the freshly boiled okro soup if he ever brought evil Biafran reports near her peaceful home. She also warned Femoo of listening to the rebels' propaganda as it was an offence to do so. It was the police who tuned in!

One day, on his way to school, he was suddenly confronted with an unusual long convoy of military vehicles. They were ambulances with the famous Red Cross symbol. It seemed some of the patients had suffered different kinds of wounds. Some appeared to have been machete or even burnt.

Later, unusual crimes started emerging from the decays of the civil war: mass rape, armed robbery, corruption and crimes, at hitherto unknown quarters. War was over by January 11, 1970. Ibo friends were back but under a different status, Femoo recalled. Giddy from

Afikpo, Benedict from Aba, all took turns as house boys at his uncle's home. The Afikpo teenager had guinea worm, the first ever seen by Femoo. He was able to learn some Ibo slangs and hear both real and imaginary war stories from his new friends.

That year Christmas Eve, two men brought a case to a land lord in the neighborhood. What happened? The south easterner, resting in bed after the hard day's work couldn't bear any longer the Hausa mallam's prayer sessions at the window of the south easterner.

The mallam explained that his fellow tenant's window was the best location facing the Kaaba, the compulsory direction for Muslims prayers. The landlord was advised to come down and relocate the Mallam otherwise; two unexpected visitors would be at heaven's gate that night. The south easterner promised to decapitate him, at prayer, and then kill himself so that he could at least have his well deserved peace. Young Femoo wondered, peace on earth, hell or in heaven?

Indeed, the Yorubas are right: it is because of previous misunderstanding that turned every song raised by the opponent into sinister proverbs.

CHAPTER 10

Dad's Death

It was a Friday that started like any other ending the working week. It even promised to be nice, nay, very eventful. Dad was expected to fete his Church group so mum had started to cook one of those special meals for about fifty members of the Revival group. Mum had gone to the recently opened Oja Oba, market, at Sabo quarter of the city, shopping for the best of seasonings: curry, magi cubes, thyme, and locust beans.

As usual, friends and relatives had rallied round to give their helping hands to mum, towards the success of the family big do. The aroma pervaded and soaked the air making even the mouth of the most insensitive passerby to water. Various mongrel and unkempt cross bread dogs stampeded and barked at one another as they jumped at bones and broth thrown out of the kitchen.

Femoo was dribbling and dodging at the nearby Police Barracks football field where some ceased accidented vehicles had been fast encroaching on the sole recreation ground. Suddenly, he felt about a dozen men closing in on him. He kicked the ball towards the goalie, surged leftwards and skillfully withdrew backwards but rightwards, thereby escaping almost all his inattentive would-be captors.

-"What's the matter?" he queried.

-"Nothing really, just let's go home!" they all chorused.

-"Then, why are you trying to catch me like a fowl, did I offend anybody?"

-"Let nobody then hold me, please", he cried out, now rather apprehensive.

By now, Femoo had begun to sweat unusually and felt his knees buckle. What was happening to him? On reaching the frontage of his home, the answers were screaming at him. There was his mum rolling on the floor, shouting "e e...Eeh, my crown is gone; I am now headless. Someone, please help me out; with six children I am now alone. Baba Ola is that what we agreed?" Sympathizers, some also in tears, were seen clumsily trying to help her up. Her wrappers, red with the clayey earth, head gears off, bare footed. It was quite an emotional scene.

From God knows where, Femoo surged forward, helped mum up and staring her in the face, he declared authoritatively: "mum, weep no more! I will help you. You won't suffer, just rise I shall do my best to support and sustain you, by God's grace". Even to his pleasant surprise, mum asked: "son, are you saying so, really?" It must have been a moment of divine inspiration. Femoo then moved into dad's bedroom and saw him in bed, he felt him, and he was still warm! Was there hope of his coming round again?

The men who brought the corpse in a Volkswagen kombi bus told of how daddy was fully packed and ready and just wanted to have a nap before joining the 5 pm lorry home. He never did again.

On reaching home, the men, in their fifties and sixties, dad's age grade, still in their farm jumpers of various colours, but mostly rumpled and tarnished with indelible green plantain and cocoa sap, didn't know how to break the news of their 54 year-old in-law's sudden death. They therefore simply told mum who was in the kitchen, that her husband had arrived from the farm. She was reported to have curtly welcomed him. She even queried him why he had delayed that much, knowing that he had a meeting to host at home. Then, came, the startling revelation...

Various relatives, from both mum and dad's branches of the family trees, neighbours and Church ministers, all came to sympathize. All rooms were packed.

Mean while there was nobody to break the evil news to granny at his own ilode residence, about four kms away. Ultimately, Femoo had to go. He tried but no taxis were either available or willing to go there. So Femoo had to trek to ilode. Granny was quietly seated on the famous petrol tank-turned seat observing, according to her words, "who is going and who is coming". As soon as he emerged, granny sprang off her seat, exclaiming:

"-Hope nothing is wrong, Femoo, my dear?"

-"Nothing", he said.

-"Of course, I can see in your steps, something has gone wrong!"

-"Why do you think something is wrong, granny?"

-"Ese ofo, ree"!, she screamed in Yoruba, meaning "this a gait of the bereaved you have!"

Both granny and Femoo headed for Moore, where she wailed and whined, mourning the untimely death of her daughter's husband.

Femoo and his siblings were taken to the house of the uncle, nearest by. He woke up confused. Why was he there? Has his daddy really died or was it a dream? He tried to wish away this night mare but it was like Naaman's leprosy stuck to Gehazi. It simply refused to go!

In the middle of the first night, in their house, dad already lying in state, Femoo gathered days later, there was a thunder storm. The tall old paw- paw tree between their house and the neighbour's was uprooted and it fell on the electric cable. In the process, the cable pulled off the facing board of the house. Many of the sympathizers were scared, some even screaming, "baba, baba, please!" one of his maternal uncle's wives, had one of these nondescript ailments that makes the victim bark and yell at night. She equally manifested.

The first seven days almost all slept there to support and comfort mummy. Food items were brought from various places. The numbers started diminishing after the seventh night according to their closeness to mum, the chief mourner.

Various advice pieces were served on mum and the children. Baba Kayode, the carpenter across the street made the coffin. He must have been paid by the appropriate branch of the family network of relations. On Sunday, 7th February, 1972, the old man was buried at the backyard, in a solemn but typically evangelical Church ceremony by the Christ Apostolic Church. The mounds of excavated red soil covered most of Femoo's just ripening beds of tomatoes.

The children moved back to their places to sleep and mum sewed black mourning frocks and gowns for school. The relatives came one dawn to finish the agenda of sharing the late man's property. Femoo recalled faintly that dad's Dane gun was the only item that a paternal uncle picked. That single act was significant. It put paid to the promise of the father to teach him how to shoot and hunt when he would come of age. No question of giving mum to any other uncle, she had declared her readiness to live the rest of her 45 years life as a widow.

The youngest, the baby of the house barely three and a half years old, was one day at the backyard, by the grave yard, with mum and Femoo. She spotted one ripe tomato fruit and picked it up calling mum to move near too. She then asked her: "when will daddy grow and give fruits?" Mum, was he not recently planted?" Mum, with her typical motherly calm, carried the baby and gently hugged her while covering her little mouth with her left palm. Mum stared at me and whispered: "Omode o mo nkan kan.O fee ye o na nigba ti oo ba nilo baba". This means, this child doesn't know anything. You will soon understand it when you will have need of a father.

The reality came fast. Mum was having insomnia, tension or pressure problems. Hospital calls and various drugs administered. She would call Femoo to pray in the dead of the night for her to be able to sleep. He would and God, in his mercies, would answer. It is not easy for one single hand to lift the load to the head. Mum had to increase the family income. Teaching with the Standard six certificate could not feed five hungry mouths of fast-growing boys and girls.

Rev. Father Fabian, the school principal, emerged near Femoo's house as an angel, one week into the mourning. He advised Femoo to return to school and quickly apply for N K Zard scholarship program. He did. It was for the whole Sate but chances based on local government. Ife then was easily the largest in Oyo state. It comprised Ile-Ife itself, Ipetumodu, Edunabon, Moro, Akinlalu Yakooyo, Sekona, Garage Olode, and even far away Ifetedo.

Why was his own local government not subdivided to better his chances as others' were? It was rumored that his Royal Highness, the Kabiyesi, had insisted on people not dividing his ancestral domain. Femoo had opted for Arts, precisely, French. It was interviews and interviews world without end. It seemed other candidates from other provinces like Ilesa and Osogbo found theirs easier. In the end he won, along his classmate, Kola, who chose science.

So school fees were out of the list of head aches, at least for Femoo. But, what about his other siblings? The principal wanted to know whether he could share Femoo's award with his brother, Ola who was beginning school. Mum replied in the negative. She wanted the winner of the scholarship to enjoy it to the fullest.

God had answered his prayers. Femoo recalled the first Holy Mass organized on a Thursday evening for the final year students of his school. He had been at the assembly hall early. The sacristan and officiating priest, the Principal himself donned their various colourful robes.

Femoo had been fasting and honing himself up for real spiritual battle in the ways that he believed the Apostolic and New Testament faith had thought him. Then came prayer time, and Femoo knelt to praise and worship God the Father and then the son...then What? The bell rang and came the perturbing responsorial: "we pray thee o Lord!"

At the next call to prayer, he decided to go faster, but it was no use the fatal bell...like the angelus... struck again and again. So Femoo followed them mechanically, ...we pray thee o lord...

Later the Rev Fr. Asked him how he found the Mass, Femoo told him his struggle to pour out his minds to God. The minister reminded Femoo that before he prayed God had heard him. Femoo, not convinced asked the Reverend what he would do if he were to be confronted with the mentally deranged people as they had at the prayer power House of the Christ Apostolic Church Moore. The man of God spoke of asylum and the will of God.

Mummy opted to train herself. It would be a two year- in-service grade two certificate course. So for about two years she braced herself up and faced the training programme squarely. Having taught for about twenty-five years, methods and concepts of teaching were not her head aches. But Algebra was! How do we multiply negative figures or even common letters of the English alphabet? Why add y plus b? Femoo, who was seating for the West African School certificate Examination, came handy. He and mum had sleepless nights, studying.

He poured out the mathematical formulae and tricks he learnt from Mr Ara, the grade one teachers certificate holder from Ife but who successfully taught Advance Level math candidates. He explained to her mum that just as her enemy's enemies would be reckoned as her friends, so should negative multiplied by negative be positive. Thus she would have: $-2 \times -2 = +4$. Likewise her enemy's friend would be an enemy as negative multiplied by positive would be negative. Thus: $+4 \times -4 = -16$.

A lot of fasting and prayers went into the preparations. She complained of some irregularities of bribery of examiners, inspectors, markers and even typists by some but she did pass.

Femoo read very, very hard. He would rise as early as 4 am even on Saturdays in order to finish the house hold chores. He would then head for the home of the best math student to solve equations till late nights, often without lunch. He would also teach others French and English languages in return. Days and nights of study succeeded one another. Smell of kerosene, red eyes, were some of the tell tale signs of hard working students, he recalled.

His uncle encouraged him with the stories of their own days as students. The best students would turban himself with wet towel, place his feet in a basin of water, all these to scare away sleep at night. Femoo didn't need to go that far to seek inspirations. He had them galore: the charms of Unife, the taunting and daunting poverty ghosts that must be laid fast and the light of divine encouragement received daily from mum. God was gracious to him! After all, is it not God that whisks off flies for the poor cow without a tail?

Femoo's WAEC results were delayed in coming. Prayers were said. Much fasting was included too. At home the order of conflict or problem resolution was clear. You asked, sought, prayed, fasted and praised God. Prophet Feso had foreseen it clearly. Femoo would be shoulder-carried by his mates when the results would be released. So it was. He had gone to school to endoss the fifty kobo or five shillings postal order that his brother had sent him from Lagos. There, students rushed at him, lifted him up, the division one aggregate 17 scholar. Femoo, son of a poor widow, had passed in division one, about the school's best results with three alphas and three high credits.

He could lift his head up, but only slightly: two other practically equally good results were there but also because daddy was no more there. The man who had at the Alapata farm predicted that Femoo would be the first man of his clan to read in the University had gone six feet below.

Tears of two different nature welled up his eyes. One of triumph, the other of loss. He would soldier on. He had found the secret. He has got the light. He will wave it to disperse the darkness threatening his lonely but pioneering way.

And as he had promised he would go ahead and reach his Jerusalem with the head of Goliath.   Some of his mates celebrated even their division two; Femoo would go to that famous University of Ife that he had vowed to go long ago in primary five. That was in 1967. He had to teach at a primary school in town in order to get funds and experience. At the end of the year, the Udoji awards came. It was a significant salary arrears dropped at his lap by providence, it was indeed.

Suddenly his salary of forty four naira doubled to ninety-six naira a month. It was five kobo for a taxi drop in

1974/5 at Ile Ife and the imported shirt was about five naira. His first Limson shoes of the platform style cost only twelve naira. Life in the oil boom years was quite nice.

Oh... talk of the Udoji salary arrears paid! Several school teachers and especially head masters lost their teeth. How? They had all purchased refrigerators. Since they were first seeing ice cubes that easily, they decided to dump so many ice cubes in their mouths. Results? Teeth came tumbling down!

The Ife general hospital also had the direct impact of the Udoji award. Many teachers had purchased motor cycles, Kawasaki, Suzuki, Honda etc. Accidents were all over. It was free fall: broken limbs, ribs, sternum and then stamina and finally broken homes.

Yes, no holds barred. Before the civil war, parents went on drinking spree. Palm wine was free, as long as an Ife man could clamber Oke Oloyibo, i.e. White man's hill, where the white man gave it free. In the evening having drunk themselves silly, Femoo would watch the drunk boast and threaten to jump off the moving taxi cab. Women, mostly illiterate, would go on their knees begging the silly fools not to kill themselves at the expense of the government. When Femoo asked dad what flushed those silly fools out of his area, daddy's reply was taciturn: civil war and higher school fees.

Is it not hunger that teaches mad man wisdom?

CHAPTER 11

The university

On Saturdays, Femoo started visiting the University of Ife Campus. After all, his distant cousin from Ilesa had taken him to the varsity Zoological gardens since he was in form three. Here they would watch lions, Patas monkeys, chimpanzee, hyenas, birds, various snakes etc. The joy of the Unife Zoo was the near natural environment in which the animals were kept.

The imposing university gate, with its Ori olokun ancient bronze head of goddess of the sea, as its emblem, was a great sense of pride to any Ife son. The close to three kilometers drive-in, embellished with colorful flowers on either sides, meticulously manicured luxuriantly green lawns, carpeting the fine edifices, were enthralling to Femoo.

He would go to the bookshop and flipped through some books. He even ordered there, a Micro Robert French dictionary from France. It was about twelve naira and it took about six weeks to arrive. There, he stumbled on a book and made an interesting discovery about how close French and Portuguese languages were. At least, these two are romance languages and therefore closer to each other, than they are to German.

He had paid and obtained admission forms for the universities of: Ife, Ibadan, Lagos, Nsukka and the youngest, Benin. He took the exams one after the other and passed them all. The Benin University didn't even require any concessional examination. Of the six universities existing in Nigeria then, the only one he did not apply to, was that of ABU, Zaria. Mum, who reluctantly allowed for Nsukka form would not grant ABU. It was too far for a widow's son of Femoo's closeness. Do you blame the widow of mum's life experience? It was barely then five years that Nigeria ended a bloody, senseless and ethnically-motivated civil war.

Femoo remembers, the day he got the Ife University admission result, he jumped for joy. He saw an uncle nearby and shared the news with him. His joy was doused. The uncle told him that people didn't usually pass at Ife and that he should remember he had no father. When he got home he told his mum. She expressed some surprise that such negative remarks could come from a younger brother she had helped, more so one who was supposed to be a minister of God. She faced the walls of her bedroom, and in tears, reported it all to God, the husband of widows. She vowed to Femoo that he would go to the university even if it meant selling off her last wrapper to pay the fees. Femoo, equally promised to do his best and get the first degree in his clan.

University Hostel!

The D-day had come, finally. It was the resumption day in September of 1975. Femoo could hardly wink throughout the night. Granny had donated from her stall, two

Moroccan Titus sardine tins and another of blue-band margarine and two loaves of bread. Pyjamas, electric torch, garri, cabin biscuits, and can/bottle openers, even coconuts from daddy's farm in Alapata: all were carefully packed. Mum had earnestly begged her uncle for his Mercedes Benz 200 car, for Femoo to be conveyed to the University of Ife. He obliged.

Femoo was posted to the great Fajuyi hall, named after the first military governor of Western Region: late Col. Adekunle Fajuyi from Iyin-Ekiti. So it was considered the hall of heroes while Awolowo hall was seen as being for the docile folks. The Post Graduate Hall was in a class of its own.

On entering the room in the basement of the hall, they found the three beds well laid, two toilet rolls placed on each of the side tables too. One was labeled 'Fay', and the other 'Lotus'. There were equally three wardrobes, two were in-built while the third was wooden, mobile and apparently improvised just as the third bed. Femoo could see that the student population explosion was setting in.

They found a middle aged fair complexioned student with an Ekiti Yoruba accent, sitting on one of the beds. He welcomed warmly mum and the itinerary from Ife. After prayers and various last minutes words of advice, mum turned to the fair complexioned man, spotting a stylish Afro cut. She appealed to him to "please take care of this your younger brother", pointing at Femoo. "But mummy", said-he, clearing his throat, "we are both beginners. Moreover here, everybody must bear his own cross".

The middle aged man still went ahead to tell mum that what he would do she would not probably recommend it for her younger son. "Here it is everyone for himself, and God for us all, the devil takes the last man" On hearing this rather disturbing comment, mum and her group made for the flush door.

On returning from seeing off his people, Femoo bounced on the bed and got immediately busy reading the University prospectus and various documents introducing clubs and societies of this his new world. While flipping through some, and partly imagining how registration would be, he repeated to himself, the roommate's words: 'here, it's everyone for himself, God for us all...the devil takes the last man' He went on his knees and decided to pray, the devil will not take him. No..., he will be for God; he will not be for the devil. He will not be the last man, either.

The middle aged man was a new comer, a JJC, Johnny just Come like him. He had entered the university with a grade two certificate earned the year that Femoo was born. He had been a free headmaster in Ibadan. He had been quite affluent in his own domain. The first night on campus showed it all. The man, made several attempts to lay his bed but failed, and then, finally, clambered into it.

What was Femoo hearing? The headmaster-turned -student was actually summoning his house helps, Sifawu, and Abeni to come and lay his bed for him on the campus. He was not done; he gave clear instruction for his two pillows to be placed correctly for his pot belly and his sleepy head! People actually came to the university for different motives. He later confessed that he had come to enhance his chances in the Action Group political party. He had complained that Chief Awolowo's party had short changed him because he had no degree after his name. Femoo had to teach him some French as a compulsory course for him!

One day, Femoo went to console his course mate at a close by hall. The young man had remained inconsolable. He had just lost his childhood girl friend to a senator, who organized thugs to also beat him to unconsciousness along Asaba road. There, another elderly headmaster from the Cross river state, riding a Volkswagen car, ordered that all lights in the room be put out at about 8 pm, for him to sleep. That also put off all consolatory or commiseration pleas of Femoo to his mate. Headmasters were heading their mates, indeed.

Registration was done promptly and lectures followed immediately. The widow's son applied himself assiduously to books and to the Bible. Indeed, the university study was an epitome of freedom. Some were serious while some would play all sorts of music, attend all parties and forgot to attend classes. Of course, the Great Unife was tough. Those who started with preliminary studies in lieu of Advanced Levels were called 001-series people. This appellation came from the codes of their courses. They were told that the first zero meant that they did not know from where they were coming, the second, that they didn't know where they were going, the final figure 1, means that their names were written only with a pencil. It was fail in one subject fail in all, and go home. Preliminary studies, as the first university year was called, were really primed guns ready to discharge!

There was also the Pyrates, secret association, whose membership was known to the initiated only. They usually began their activities about mid night, drank heavily, and wore black uniforms. They restricted their activities to the football pitch.

Promiscuity was visible. Recklessness among lecturers abusing students was not uncommon. A lecturer in Chemistry was notorious for demanding sex gratification for female students to pass his course, usually compulsory for almost all science students. He would reportedly perch on the critical path of the students, on the natural sciences building, as a predator hawk, and from there, stalk and shoot down unsuspecting young female students.

One elderly student, having children clamoring at home for his graduation, was reportedly tired of failing a course without clear reasons, one day decided to solve his problem in his own way. What did he do? He bought a machete and headed for the notorious lecturer's quarters. There he spent hours daily just sharpening the machete. Once in a while he would raise his head up, and brandish the machete in the air, attempt to cut the air, and shout: "sure this is not sharp enough to do this big job, is it?" The wife and children of the lecturer were worried at just seeing a student stooping in their garden, honing a machete from morning till evening. They garnered bits of courage still lingering on their minds and asked the man why so much time sharpening a machete.

The man casually responded that there was nothing for them to worry about. That since it seemed that Dr. (mentioning their bread winner's name) had become so heartless to him; this machete should help him further to become headless too. Of course the wife and the children got the essence of the message. The man passed his reseat exam.

At the modern European languages department, with three quarters female, lectures were really a parade of latest French fashion. Other students could sometimes steal in to watch the cat walk-like array of students' attire. Various gimmicks were utilized to catch girl or boy friends during what was called the 'Great October rush'.

There was the case of a lady, really maverick, she would wait until lectures began, then she would walk in striking the terrazzo faculty of humanities floor. As if that were not enough, she would insist on sitting opposite where most males sat and scatter her legs till they could effortlessly see whatever was under her skirts. If all these were gimmicks to catch lecturers, it was a total fiasco. She failed woefully and had to repeat the year.

There were the good aspects of this varsity life too. For instance, Femoo could read French newspapers like 'Le Figaro' French magazines, almost on the same day of publication. French films were brought, on a weekly basis, practically, to French and francophone students by special arrangements with the French Embassy in Lagos.

Oh... there were annual bursary awards! These were either given on the basis of courses like incentives to education students by the Federal Government or by State Governments to their students. Loans were equally available subject to proper bonding. The Governments of Bendel and Rivers states had the highest awards. Their students, mostly also on loans, bought the most sophisticated radio/cassette players and latest motorcycles like the Halley Davison hybrid machines costing about one thousand five hundred naira. Such machines could easily overtake Peugeot 504 on the Ife/Ibadan express way. Some even helped in test driving such vehicles driving as far as Jos, Benue plateau State, in the middle belt region of Nigeria.

There were also the special Government scholars! These were students from African countries struggling for Independence such as Angola, Mozambique, South Africa and Zimbabwe. Many of them were so spoilt or drunk with funds or fun that they drank themselves to stupor. One of them in Femoo's course of Portuguese even got pregnant.

Aside from the Main female hostel named Moremi, the Yoruba heroine, the latest female hostel annex was tagged Mozambique while the male annex was called Angola. Femoo recalled those were the days of Nigeria's high profile African liberation Foreign policy driven by the military government of Generals Murtala Mohammed/Olusegun Obasanjo.

Some other students from indigent states could thank God for about 500-naira annual bursary award. Governors like Chief Bola Ige of Oyo state gave Femoo his first five-hundred-naira cash. Why would he not thank God? The breakfast of bread, egg and tea or coffee cost about ten kobo while lunch or dinner, twenty –five kobo only. Even at graduation the salary might not be more than three hundred naira a month.

Femoo would spend hours at the cricket pavilion with the CAC Bethel, in prayers and deep theological studies, under Prof Malomo Mevbrel. Many testimonies of answered prayers were visible landmarks brought from those prayer and worship sessions. The only physical pains were the Sunday lunch missed by the Bethelites. Oh yes! On Sundays, the lunch was special: joloff rice, drum sticks, (i.e.chiken thighs) ice cream with fruit salad as alternative. Students even had choice of special diets without spices.

Even the aroma, taste and fame of the University Sunday lunch attracted non students from Ile – Ife town. Usually the sermon, especially under prophetess Oluranti could run on for three to four hours! Consequences were: closing morning services at 5 pm. Of course, the sumptuous lunch is missed!

Femoo had a course mate, called Newman Hope, of Izon ethnic extraction, and erroneously called Ijaw by the British colonial authorities. His Izon names: Ayauge Ebiakpo. He had been with his parents to the Gold Coast, now Ghana in search of the El Dorado. He had a very sound education but had serious attacks of migraine that prevented him from serious swotting. That was a setback indeed for a student of modern European languages where fat novels were prescribed as broad spectrum drugs in a general hospital by our far eastern physicians even before patients opened their mouth.

Newman, at his wit's end of consulting fake and real healers, one day, persuaded by Femoo, tried the C. A. C. prayer sessions on the campus and was miraculously healed. He became a fervent worker. He thereafter became very close to Femoo who later learnt about Newman's life odyssey. His friend's mother, Koru, whose name means hope, from Ekeremor, western part of the Rivers State, married to Ebuoiwe, a delta Izon across the sea, had complained to Femoo. She moaned the coming of the European oil mongers who poisoned the sea and killed all the fishes of her land.

Newman's mother had wondered what kind of a life an Izon mother could lead if she could no longer dive into the river and bring out the fresh fishes or paddle a few miles and bring home seafood for her children.

Reading Femoo's blank face, his friend Newman tried to explain the irony of the modern day plight of the riverine community in Nigeria: the national wealth was gradually adversely affecting their way of life. Femoo scanned the sky for signals. Suddenly on that day, the first rain of the year, with hail stone, fell on Ile- Ife, the cradle of the Yoruba. Could the heavens be protesting the treatment of their children on earth?

In the mid 70s, the University of Ife was indeed very proactive having courses that had direct impact on the society. One professor from the University of Ibadan, the pioneer of Nigerian Universities founded in 1948, described the University of Ife as "the Cinderella of Nigerian Universities". And so it was that the university was the only one offering Portuguese language, a course in which Femoo excelled. So he was chosen with three other course mates to help teach English to Portuguese-speaking Angolan soldiers in Ilorin, Nigerian Army School.

As instructors, they were quartered and treated as senior army officers. They had night guards; they were chauffer-driven and could have subsidized drinks and meals at the mess. Oh the mess was a very interesting experience of the balanced social life for the senior Army officers. Games and sports were strictly observed.

Femoo had one summer holiday, followed the CAC student's Association, to their special Holiday camp at Oniyere in Ibadan where he was baptized in the

Holy Spirit. His life changed dramatically: he became much fervent, in faith, prayer and Bible.

Thank God for his mercies! After a competitive exam, the widow's son qualified for French scholarship in France in partial fulfillment of his first degree in French language. Finally it was time to go, passport was acquired at Ibadan, visa from the French Embassy in Ikoyi Lagos and off they went on a DC 10, UTA French airlines flight.

His other colleague fellow scholar, Ossy, from Imo state, and Femoo were as excited to be airborne for the first time in their life. They saw houses like match boxes, express roads like ant paths in the village.

CHAPTER 12
IN FRANCE

Once in France, they had to go to Paris where every administrative action began in those days. All documentation done in Paris, the duo headed for a taxi stand. What did they find? There were, as taxi cabs Citroen, Mercedes Benz and other big cars used by only multi-millionaires back home in Nigeria.

Then, began, the ride on the TGV; high-tech French train. The speed was terrific, hence its name, 'Train a Grand Vitesse', TGV, meaning High Speed Train. They finally arrived in the city of Grenoble, in the south eastern Rhone-Alps department of France. They met other students from all over the world, including other scholars from the other five Nigerian universities. Mostly were scholars except Nsukka students who came on their university arrangements.

Studying in France was highly educative, not only because of the phonetics of the French language, by the best native speakers. There was also the direct experience of a developed country's modus operandi laid bare to them. There was the humane social security system that took care of the weaker class of the society too. The ageing European societies were becoming visible, and the structures of the European Economic Community, EEC, were just being confirmed in 1978/79.

He saw the desk top computer as routine office equipment in the Universite 3 de Grenoble. Back at Unife, only the elite computer students who could speak the computer language, punch cards were hallowed enough to visit the almighty computer. We heard that it was as big as the whole room. Only God knows who had ever seen it!

On the first Sunday morning, in October, Femoo donned his colourful traditional 'Aso Oke' garment, and headed for what he thought a nearby Church. He walked and walked but no church was in sight. He trekked till his palms were red and biting, his ears were hard and fast becoming numb with cold. His ears were so frost-bitten that he felt touching them would make the ear lobes to crumble like over exposed bread crust!

When, suddenly, he sited a building with young men, trooping in. He also turned in. The young men were excited but not for long. Was it the red alaari (crimson) garment, made at Oke- Ijan quarters of Ife that attracted them, or the colour of his dark African skin? Perhaps, both. Femoo, sizing them up as they drank and smoked, asked for a Protestant church, at least not to go too deep into Pentecostalism.

The French boys burst into hysterical laughter, rolling over. "Young man!" they exclaimed, "Protestantism is it a political pressure group or what?" He went into theological history, but the boys were as deaf as door posts. They invited the African student to come and drink. They submitted that Sundays were for sports or merry making. Was Femoo beginning to see the sordid reality that led Europe and the Western Democracy to their current state of moral bankruptcy?

Continuing his search, he discovered an old Orthodox Church near the Verdun Square. At the end of the service Femoo was warmly welcomed for helping to reduce the average age of the handful worshippers from about 80 years! An old lady told him the story of how Christianity used to be the leading factor in shaping the morality of their homes. Femoo never returned to the octogenarian Church again

He went through a Canadian fellowship where much of history and wine cum Holy Communion were taken than of Christ. The search continued. One day, four ladies one from Abraka college of Education and the two from Nsukka, and one from Unilag, were brought to Femoo. Those who brought them complained that they would neither dance nor drink: they were SUs, (read, serious, uncompromising, practicing Christians) so only Femoo could understand them!

Indeed, he understood them. They had been frustrated for not finding a living Church in the city of Grenoble, France. They all discovered the Assemblies of God, Cours Beriat street. At long last! It was like a travel - weary soul discovering an oasis in the desert. They all sat down to drink deep at the well of life and feed on the bread of life. It was a season of excitement. French Pentecostals, speaking in tongues, in Ibo language without having ever been to Africa. Femoo's Ibo-speaking sisters were so excited they almost hit the tall roof of the church.

Practically the teenagers would come to relate unending stories of nightmares, somebody possibly maltreating their mothers in Nigeria, their fathers probably involved in accidents back home. Femoo would listen and soak in all their worries, fears and fright, like a dry sponge dropped in a bath tub of their thoughts. In the end, he would pray for them and the rituals proved therapeutic. Yes all he had to do was listen, and exclaim appropriately:" hun!, what a shame, oh my God!"

One day one of his Christian sisters asked Femoo to relate to them too, his dreams and fears. He said there was no need, but when they insisted, he told them just one. The previous night, he had a dream that he was slaughtered, hacked into pieces, and   packed into a big basket. The ladies screamed and recoiled in horror. They yelled: "And what happened?" Femoo told them he just rose in prayer and declared that such dream was not for him. It was from Satan. He commanded it to return to the pit of hell where it belonged. He capped it with the famous Pentecostal declaration: "I shall not die but live and declare the glory of the Lord" (Ps 118: 17).

Lectures were deep and hard but Femoo decided to do his best. In France, Professors boasted of the numbers of PhD students they had trained not that they have failed as some of their counterparts did back home.

Then came the final year exams, and Femoo came tops of all the 280-strong international student groups, with his name written in the Honours board as the best performance ever by a Nigerian! Some of the students of the college of education were wiser. Although they merely managed a pass, they were wise to have stayed one year extra, and obtained a Master's degree from France.

Back in the university, the final year at Ife was hectic: thesis, external examiners. Of course the irregularities in the academic examination system had not vanished over night just because Femoo was away to France in 1978.

There were the riots of all the Universities over withdrawal of meal subsidies. Breakfast jumped from ten kobo to twenty and lunch and dinner jumped from ten kobo to twenty. So in a day, three square meals would now cost seventy kobo. Some even vowed it had jumped by a hundred per cent to one naira, fifty kobo per day! Unife took the lead with hunger strike. They were cordoned off and within four days scarcity of food set in. Various symptoms started manifesting. It was the "Ali Mon go!" riots, corrupt form of "Ali must go!" protesting that Col. Ahmadu Ali, the physician and then minister of Education should resign.

It happened that the head of State, General Olusegun Obasanjo was visiting Ife campus with his old school mate, Prof. Ojetunji Aboyade, the erudite professor of economics and vice chancellor of the University. So the Military head of State addressed the student asking them to be, among other things, "responsibly irresponsible".

A session of Student 'congress' was held at the sports centre. An Ogun state lady student was commanding the masses. It was believed that her green skirt had been "soaked" in African power concoction. Femoo, a convinced socialist, was among those at the fore front. They had crossed the sports centre stretch of the beautiful university drive in, when he heard the clear voice, "Femoo go back, you will gain nothing from these demonstrations. In fact, lives will be lost" He heeded immediately. He tried to explain to a few but was treated as a coward.

He now faced his Bible reading and finished the whole Bible for the first time. Femoo's life was altered. It happened as he had received from the divine voice. Lives and much property were ruined all over the country. Universities were shut down and opportunists took over the demonstrations. While Femoo was back home, secondary and primary schools pupils lost their lives in the riots. It became an immense national crisis.

Recruitment into the civil Service was done by officers in various universities. Femoo filled the form and seeing the chance of being trained in Geneva, opted for the post of Information Officer, external Publicity section. On his way from the Students' union Building he heard the inner voice to change the post to that of External Affairs Officer. He obeyed.

Femoo had prayed and summoned his most holy faith and hoped that the Grace of Christ would do the rest. It did. They were interviewed in batches of four or six candidates. He was the only undergraduate; all the others were completing their Masters in International Relations, a course in which Unife was about the oldest and most famous in Nigeria.

The widow's son was undaunted, God was on his side. After all, He made him choose this course which nobody from the ancient city of Ile- Ife had ever been before him. The questions came, flying: "what is the capital of Zimbabwe?" The news of Change of name from 'Salisbury' to 'Harare' just filtered in to Femoo at the 7 o'clock radio Nigeria news that morning! All the others except one missed it. The other who knew it, being of heavy Yoruba accent swallowed the 'h' sound of 'Harare' thus, miraculously offering Femoo, a bonus mark to start with. Then, came the general appearance aspect. One of the candidates came in shirt and trousers, not even a tie did he wear. Femoo had come in a three-piece grey velvet suit; the only one he had purchased in Grenoble, worth show casing.

Then, came, practically, all other questions of French origin, such as the meaning of 'CD', CORPS DIPLOMATIQUE. Femoo licked them easily as he would the African pap with Akara (fried bean cakes) balls.

He got posted to the old Anambra State for the compulsory National youth service for one year. While he shrugged it off as any post like others, his siblings and especially his mum could barely sleep. The only saving grace was that the previous year his age-long friend, Eddy had survived being posted across the river Niger, the land of the Ibos. Oh that year relatives came to console Mama

Eddy for his son's imminent departure to the land of the cannibals, so they assumed.

So Femoo journeyed east wards. He crossed the famous Niger Bridge at Onitsha, saw the breath-taking canyon near Enugu, popularly called the Milking hill.

The NYSC training camp was at Nsukka, in the north of the state. It was a Para-military training. Early morning drills, physical training, military language at parades. There were regimental Sergeant Majors, squadron leaders. Orders were barked out such as 'SQUAD, SQUAD SHON', for 'SQUAD ATTENTION'and 'AJUWAYA' for 'AS YOU WERE'

For primary assignment, Femoo was posted to the Anambra Broadcasting Corporation ABC 1, Enugu. However, despite his highly rated microphone voice, for lack of accommodation, he could not serve there. He returned to the NYSC, secretariat and got picked by a desperate school principal, to teach. Half way to the school, the principal, from Onitsha, suddenly exclaimed "but you are a man!". Femoo, in his mind only, was answering "yes madam, do I look like a lady, with my well grown beard and side burns?"

Later her fears were allayed as Mrs. Anya found out that Femoo was a fervent Christian. He was in fact, too serious about his purity and holistic spirituality in sanctity to toil with sexual promiscuity. How can? (He could hardly shake hands with his university female sisters, to avoid infatuation) His prayers were so different from the orthodox recitals that the Abakpa Nike girls started calling him in Ibo, Onye nkuzi, n'afa Jesus, that is; 'teacher, Mr. In Jesus name'

Evangelical crusades on week-ends took Femoo and his Christian youth corpers group to Opuje in the northernmost boundary with Benue State, where the Ibo man also required an interpreter. They went to Atani, in

Ogbaru local government in the riverine southern part, the home of the famous musician, Osita Osadebe.

There was a clear evidence of fetish worship in Atani. Even miniature houses were constructed for their idols. At the city gate was suspended, on a looping horizontal bar, a slaughtered white goat, bloated but dripping blood from its mouth on nearly all vehicles that crossed the gate! The day of the crusade, after three days of fasting and prayers, was the d-day, indeed. In the nearby, primary school, Femoo was leading the prayer band in a prayer chain. Then came the rain, thunder bolt, torrents... the prayer never stopped, and no discouragement.

At the end, the Okpara, the crowned prince of the village, was converted: he was moved at the determination, the unwavering faith of the preacher, Brother Felix A., who spoke through the rain.

Then there were those efforts by Femoo to do graduate studies in the USA. He had to do Test of English as a Foreign Language, TOEFEL form and demonstration tapes were obtained for twenty-one naira which converted to twenty-three US dollars. And all transactions were done at the Okpara Avenue post Office in Enugu.

Of course Femoo passed the test at over 600 points although he only studied for about one month. However, he could not study in the United States as he couldn't find one person to guarantee him at Ife. Even though the Florida State University and some others offered him graduate assistantship and jobs as Portuguese and French interpreters, he could not travel.

The National service was completed. The valedictory service was a day of rewards indeed. Femoo was overwhelmed with gifts that he had to charter an Urvan mini bus van from Enugu to Ife.

One of the most interesting, bus rides was the more or less eight hour one from Enugu to Ife. Femoo was bent on studying the Bible throughout but for the disturbance of the only passenger with him. It was this mama Ijesa, the owner of the chartered bus, who had moved to Enugu since 1968, with the civil war, in order to run a popular local restaurant called "mama put"

She insisted on knowing what topic could engage Femoo's attention so much. He, therefore wanting to terminate her curiosity, decided to read the passage to her straight from the Bible as in 1 Corinthians 10: 8 " Neither let us commit fornication, as some of them committed, and fell in one day three and twenty thousand". Mama Ijesa, member of the indigenous white garment churches, argued that it was not possible for a child of God to commit fornication as long as such sexual relationship was done within the Church. She said that she had based her argument on 2 Corinthians6: 14, that Christians be not unequally yoked with unbelievers. She believed that once the affair is done with believers, it was acceptable.

Femo analyzed that her idea was from the pit of hell. He argued that fornication, with whomsoever it be committed, is a terrible sin. In fact it should not be named among Christians as in Eph 5: 3. Actually fornication, or its Siamese brother or sister, adultery, are in the first and second positions of the works of the flesh rated above idolatry, or even witchcraft in the sixth position of (Gal 5: 19/20) ranking of evil.

Femoo alighted at Ife and did a thanksgiving service for a successful new chapter of life.

CHAPTER 13
Wild World of Gorillas

Femoo was admitted into the Foreign office in Lagos. One of the lecturers, a brother in his church at the University of Ife, despised it as nomadic life. Perhaps, being a natural scientist, he feared that the young man would be on perpetual motion according to Newton's law of motion. Or was he afraid Femoo will be thrown into chaotic motion like the atom?

After a few running around for documentation, first at the Civil service Commission, Federal Secretariat, Ikoyi, Lagos, then NYSC, Babs Animashahun, Surulere, the group of about seventy new appointees, headed for the Ministry of External Affairs, Marina, Lagos.

At the registry, new officers were busy doing and outdoing one another to be in the front of the documentation queue. Femoo had been surrendering his position when an old Ibo-speaking Executive Officer asked him to stop that because whoever registered before him would become his senior for life. At least, could be, during the expected 35 years of professional life, barring any accident. After some administrative hesitations, it was decided that Femoo's set of officers would pioneer the Foreign Service Academy, so it was.

The young officers were very restive as they told anybody who cared to listen that they were about the only set that would not be posted after two years of being employed. The government of generals Buhari and Tunde Idi Agbon, that took over from General Ibrahim Badamasi Babangida in December 1983, came in while Femoo was already serving abroad. He wedded Ade, an Ijebu lady, who was in the same church with him at the University of Ife, in the Swiss cold country of the Alps.

Professional Life as a young officer, under the military regime, was quite exciting, as almost all directives or decisions were either with immediate effect or people retired. There were massive retirements of public officers, including Foreign Service Officers, "with immediate effect", in those days. Femoo's senior colleagues affected had to leave their Children in his custody to enable them conclude their studies.

The Swiss were highly predictable in their policies and politics but in social life their capital city was extremely as cold as the alpine winter that lashes the city. For the Africans and others who could not ski or do winter games, the whole world seemed to have come to a stand still in winter. The only movement awaited was practically that of the bear in its famous pit, called baren graben to announce the transition from or into winter or spring He recalls that the Swiss capital, Berne, was named after the polar animal, bear.

While Femoo was excited practicing all that he had learnt at the Nigerian Foreign service academy in Lagos, his wife, still bubbling with youthfulness, was bored almost stiff. While Femoo would come for the one hour lunch break on the tram, learning and reading Latin, through the 15 minutes daily trip, his wife would prepare whatever she could improvise for African meals. She could fry bananas instead of plantain to serve as dodo, her husband's favourite meal, and match potatoes in place of yam.

When out of exuberance and enthusiasm, one day Femoo tried to skip lunch break, his wife solemnly begged him not to try it. She explained it would mean sentencing her to an unending jail term of silence and winter cold. He understood: marriage, which literally means becoming a husband in French, is essentially keeping a person's company, faithfully, and caring for him or her in all circumstances. The husband's twenty minutes lunch break time with his wife, in a cold, foreign city could make the world of a difference to an African house wife. She had invoked the first law of marriage: companionship!

Married life is another chapter in any couple's life. However, it also faces another challenge when they are married abroad and living among another group of Nigerians from various parts of the country with diversified culture and view points. Team spirit or esprit de corps had become de rigueur, absolutely a sine qua non, for survival .This law will hold true either in the Swiss winter or in the Sahara desert of Algeria.

There were internecine professional squabbles, mostly borne out of jealousies, pride, prejudices and ego problems. There were also cases of simply poor home training that embarrassed or rather betrayed some officers ...Femoo would not be involved in all these. He had learnt that fear of God, with a generous dab of faith in Him served on a dish of good home training can always stand one in good stead. The Arabs have a proverb that if your father is onion and your mother garlic, how can you their child smell fine?

His language competence had stood him in good stead. His relentless quest for le mot juste, the right word, had paid off. He, the widow's son, the boy, who had no connection, had become a diplomat of the Federal Republic. What? He had been able to stand not before mean men, as the Bible says, but in the highest summit; speaking with the President of his nation. Nay, he had been speaking with the presidents of nations. Indeed, proverbs 22: 29 still rings true even today, thus "Seest thou a man diligent in his business? he shall stand before kings; he shall not stand before mean men."

Femoo had been wondering for forty or fifty years, what he had been. Had he been an actor, a spectator or a participant observer? Or was he a mere professional, a technocrat playing his role. Or may be he had simply placed himself in the mighty hand of God to gently guide, and glide him through. Perhaps that was it.

Was it a dream or a vision that Femoo had? A well maintained zoo full of gorillas of different species and age groups. These gorillas were special breed; they were the cynosure of all other animals. The rule was to let out one champion of these Difa type to have a duel with animals in the open jungles.

The first group was well trained in various techniques and crafts of warfare. Each time the well trained set of gorillas went out to fight they would give TKO – meaning Technical Knock Out; to the other camp. They were the toast of all.

With time, age started catching up with them and the over all impact of the various duels of yester years started telling on them. They started having symptoms of altsheimer and Parkinson diseases. Moreover, the zoo keepers were no longer devoted. They started cheating on the feeds and paid little or no attention to the prime gorillas. Some had various degrees of amnesia. The young Difa gorillas were no longer sent for training at the experts villages any more.

Moreover, in their cage, younger gorillas were coming of age and were agitating vigorously to be given a chance to represent the group in external duels. The older ones won't hear any of that. Mature gorillas were getting frustrated. Some even died of heart attacks or simply collapsed.

Animals will be animals! The older gorillas would beat and bash the younger but more versatile ones. Soon a commotion developed into an internecine civil war among the Difa gorillas. Their opponents, who had envied their specialized look and training, and bright future, started jubilating.

Well, Prophets like Amos wondered aloud in Amos 7:5, "O Lord GOD, cease, I beseech thee: by whom shall Jacob arise? For he is small". Really, by whom shall this specie of Jacob arise? The friends of Jacob are too few. Worse still, these few friends are not united in purpose! Indeed, these gorillas were being attacked from all sides.

Sennacheribs were sent to them as prefects. Some were academically titled but spiritually demented, so it seemed to Femoo. Criminally minded captains cum prefects were predators, wolves but engaged as guards. But aren't the gorillas too small for these devouring locusts and worms?

What happened next was a gradual decimation and elimination of the Difa gorillas. The inconceivable had been embarked upon; younger gorillas were being sacrificed and virile and versatile ones are being sent to their untimely death. Their captains and prefects started negotiating with the opponents to represent them in duels. The Difa gorillas now concentrated on fratricidal warfare and casualties were very high in their cage. The master zoo keeper had wondered aloud on what to do.

The last time Femoo heard of the famous Difa gorillas, they were seeking prayers for their very survival. Some people believe that they had not been fortunate to have good captains or prefects. Others believe that some of their captains were either pathologically lazy or had ego problem or even had been affected by some nondescript diseases.

These gorillas had been endangered specie but only not yet so classified, officially. The Almighty had spoken. Let the gorillas be reorientated while their captains and prefects should be re-examined. Their jobs are far too serious to be awarded like a casual day contract assignment. Divided we fall, in unity we stand. More so, our people say that if the internal death does not kill, the external one can't either.

Femoo remembered his dad's famous proverb about the story of the cock and the fox. Also as he grew up reading through his daddy's old classics in Yoruba, he learned that the fox used to fear and tremble at the site of the red comb on the cock's head, thinking it was fire. So each time the cock passed by, the fox would run for its life. However, one day, the cock called the fox aside and explained to it that the comb on its head was not fire but flesh. The fox made for the flesh and the cock jumped for life begging that should its comb be pulled off it would die.

Too bad, the fox had learned the secret that it needed. Since that time the fox had always pursued and killed the cock and all its descendants.

Such is life: always keep carefully and even jealously, that which you have lest people take away your crown and fire! The Almighty has warned that holy things should not be given to dogs nor pearls be cast to the swine lest they trample on them and even turn to attack you. Have the Difa pearls and goodness not been given to the dogs and swine?

CHAPTER 14
The Havoc or Hope?

On several occasions, Femoo had taken his children to the Brazilian zoo in Brasilia. Various animals were caged there. There were the carnivores like lions, tiger, cheetah, leopards and even the puma. There were gorillas too. Special Latin American species as well as outlandish ones, imported or brought in under exchange programme, were also available. There was the elephant, adopted by the senior citizens of Brasilia, as it was assumed to be, biologically reckoning, in its eighties. Many other animals were adopted and taken care of by companies and different organizations. Such companies, embassies or civil societies had their names written on a plaque and installed in front of the cage or den of such animals.

Femoo had been telling his children about the African elephant euphemistically called in Yoruba, Ajanaku. He had told them how philosophically the African elephant is regarded as the only one capable of shaking the African Forest to its roots. The massive animal would not need anybody to build a road for it, as its passage would make the way. Like the Almighty God, wherever the elephant faces is the way!

This is awesome power at its best! The ever inquisitive girl, Olu, asked her dad:

- "do they also adopt zoo animals in Nigeria?"

Femoo scanned the blue summer sky, as if for an answer, and then stared at the red Brazilian soil. He shrugged off an answer, "quite a brilliant one, dear, not sure we're doing that yet at home, but we can try it, can't we?"

He had boasted to the young ones that the University of Ife zoo was by far better as it was conceived as closely as possible to the natural habitats of all the animals. The children, just as the Lord says, believed their father. So they awaited with anxiety, the day that they would visit the great Ife zoo.

That day came sooner than expected. Femoo was posted back home. As usual then, Lagos was the first port of call. Most of the children, having been born Lagosians and having lived in Lagos before, were not so excited at the old capital of Nigeria. They took a cursory look at its more complicated traffic jam, popularly termed 'go slow'. They watched with some undeclared disgust, or is it some shock or rather consternation, boldly written on their young faces, various attempts at survival of their fellow country men and women.

They had heard stories of highly efficient intra city and intercity urban transport services. They had heard of the LMTS buses, and the Grey hound bus services, courteous conductors, in well starched uniforms, that used to move nearly as perfect as clock work in punctuality. They were also told of neat and nice-looking bus stops.

Now back home, and with eyes wide open to see and discern, they seem to read a completely different or opposite script in this melodrama of survival of their people. Has someone switched the scripts? Or have they turned the wrong corner or entered the wrong theatre hall?

The younger Femoos seem to ask everywhere they go: "why are things like this?" "Are we home or some funny fellows had played some tricks on us or on our people and land?" One may wonder why all these questions on these young minds? Isn't it our people that also say that anybody that asks questions is doing so because he or she wants answers?

Just what did these youngsters see? Well, it seems they saw some differences over time and places. They had seen unending traffic jams that pinned them down for two solid hours and afterwards the ordeal just fizzled as if nothing ever was! They had seen commercial motorcyclists conveying three persons, including a pregnant woman, among whom one passenger is balancing, with both hands on his or her head, a calabash or plastic container of merchandise.

They had been privileged or is it trapped into entering the locally built city bus called, molue. Not only were the seats too clustered for comfort of passengers, almost every part was spiked with nails jutting out to wreck havoc at garments of passengers. Overcrowding was almost the norms. Or were they all out to confirm the song of late Afro musician, Fela Anikulapo Kuti about 99 standing and twenty sitting? As if that were not enough, any item was permitted in provided you could pay. One day a surveyor boy had brought in his material directly from the fields with all the stench of human faeces lashing at the faces of passengers. Those who could not stand or sit with it held their noses. Others simply resigned to the common fate and just drank in the waft of stench freely offered to the whole world.

Both the drivers and their mates cum conductors, usually high on local spirits, (called *ogogoro,* meaning the pinnacle) and excessive dose of malice, could unleash their repressed and primed bomb of their foul words on anybody that tried to reason with them. These youngsters had heard the drivers warning whether a passenger's panel of a head was showing red signals. The driver, who had also threatened to tap from the passenger's side, his blood as he would palm wine, was just simply refusing to look for small changes for anybody! Here the customer is not always right. The conductor is often heard shouting on top of his head, "no branching either at Yaba or Oyingbo, its to osa, that is to the Lagoon straight!" Indeed, some of these local buses have ended into the Lagoon straight. Perhaps the spirit of *olokun,* goddess of the river had possessed them.

Imagine the *molue* caught in a traffic jam, overcrowded, smokers puffing out, under the scotching

115

tropical sun of Lagos, and you are faced with both preachers and local advertisers at each other's throat in the same bus. Suddenly the traffic jam fizzled and the driver attempted to speed off when his gear lever pulled out! Previously you were being delayed now you are grounded!

Well, Femoo was able to disperse from his children's mind the negative impressions above. How? The seat of Federal government had moved to Abuja to create a better environment for all.

At the Ife zoo

With pride, Femoo took his children to see the pride of Africa, the Cinderella of Nigerian universities. They had returned to Ife the previous night in his air-conditioned *tokunbo* (imported second hand vehicle, literally it means, from overseas) Mercedes Benz car.

The long drive- in boulevard was still there. The flower beds, bare with the scotched earth cracked all over. Femoo recalled his glorious drive in here during his graduation ceremony. His uncle, Olajuba had challenged his mother while she had underplayed such a historic occasion. Since they were producing the first university graduate of their clan, he felt traditional musicians should have been hired to lead the triumphant entry.

Why not? Uncle, a successful cocoa farmer, although seen as illiterate in English, could interpret every sound, tone, and tune of the Yoruba talking drums, called *gangan*. In the past funeral ceremonies where Uncle

Olajuba as expected joined his half-sister, Femoo's mother, he had expressed his shock at learning that, Femoo, an undergraduate of the highest institution of learning, could neither hear the voice of the traditional talking drum nor dance to its rhythm.

It was quite funny.

Uncle was dancing to the drum bats. Suddenly, he stopped and headed for the neck of the chief drummer. He collared him and exclaimed, 'so if I had not done the traditional ceremonies of my mother that died fifteen years ag. Is that your headache?'

Femoo was baffled. When did the drummer say so.

The answer did not take long. Uncle shouted, *'E ma gba mi o!'* (please help me) This tattered drummer kept taunting me for not buying even a keg of palm wine to bury my aged mother and accusing me of always drinking kegs of palm wine at other people's funeral ceremonies!'

Femoo, puzzled, was cross-examining his Europeanized mind as to who is really the illiterate, him or his uncle?

They headed for the zoo. When they reached the lion's cage, they or rather Femoo and his wife, were shocked to the marrow. It was overgrown. Was the carnivore sleeping or hibernating? Not at all. One of the few remaining zoo workers declared that the lions were slaughtered to relieve them of hunger as the university authorities could no longer afford the costs of feeding them. Most of the animals were gone.

They could only see the venomous snakes hidden under their old rocks while the aged tortoise, rugged as ever and patient in hunger, stared at the family. It did not even blink once. Indeed, it seemed that the preacher was right. He had once explained in Femoo's church that the tortoise could live as long as 300 years because it is never worried or hurried and it would eat whatever it could find on the ground. How he wished mankind could do the same! But can they?

Cousins related to Femoo, the tales of woes. He heard of overcrowded Student hostels, cult havocs, and various atrocities by both students and lecturers. Worse still, librarian friends told Femoo of how students tear off relevant pages of books so that others would not compete with them. What do we call that, moral decadence or mere wickedness?

Alma Mater

For Femoo and his wife it was a baptism of shame and disappointment. He would redeem his people's image somewhere else. He decided to take the children to his alma mater, the beautiful St John's Catholic Grammar School, Ife.

The window panes were all shattered, the walls all smudged. Even trees had been cut down, not to talk of flowers. Everywhere looked as if raided and ravaged by wicked warriors avenging enemy attacks.

Oba, the old palm wine taper was once drunk when Femoo was in form three. He jumped up and started running round the field. He must have made about 12 rounds, totaling three kilometers, before he slumped. He was revived by the combined efforts of the school infirmarian and the school red cross society members.

When asked why he did that, he had explained in his broken Yoruba that he felt he also could be as good an athlete as the young students.

He explained it all. Or at least almost all: the government had taken over the school and immediately the unexpected happened. There was a riot at school. On hearing this, Femoo nearly fainted. Riots in St John's Catholic Grammar School, how could that have happened?

Worse still, he and his children can no longer stay overnight at the famous farm, Alapata. What happened? They were told that the over ten years of local armed struggles between the Ifes and their neighbouring Modakeke brothers had scared both parties away from working or sleeping overnight on their farms. Those who dared had suffered from miscreants who raided and ravaged their people and properties. So Cocoa, the tree of wealth, as his granny used to call it, has also been assaulted?

However, there was a ray of hope: Femoo's 1972 class painting still remained intact in the school dining hall. But can paintings turn or challenge realities? The great prophet Bajide had exclaimed that a powerless prophet is a painted fire, he cannot burn! He has another idea.

Femoo and family headed for Abuja, the new Federal Capital Territory of Nigeria, about five hundred and fifty kilometers away from Ile-Ife, the cradle of the Yorubas. There, they would see manicured lawns, well planned streets, orderly traffic movement and God willing, different species of drivers and passengers too, etc, etc...

The children were all eager to see the new land of hope for their generation. They have dreams...They have hope...They have plans...aspirations.

On reaching the land of New Hope, they will flutter around the petals of the flowers of hope, as beautiful butterflies in the tropical sun. They could skip like the kids atop the hills of liberty. Or could they not even choose to be freer like kids skipping atop the hills of liberty.

May be they could also soar higher as the colourful African weaver birds, free to choose the strands of leaves and strengths of branches to build their parental nests. They are so thirsty to drink fully of the nectar of the new life in the new Federal Capital. They will write their colleagues and relatives about the opening petals of new hope, democracy and advancement. Till then...

...till not so long. Why? The mother bird of time will not take so long to hatch her golden eaglets of modern times. Yes, Femoo himself now knows that his children have taught and proved day by day that the dark clouds of despair shall not be so long overcast. The sunshine of new age is rising at the internet speed, dispersing and devouring every blockade and bogy of darkness and separation.

Yes, the Yorubas of the 60s in Nigeria had almost foreseen it all, *ayelujara*, they called their colonial penny copper coin, meaning the world is interconnected. Now Femoo's children can type at an astronomical speed, converse with foreign friends on the internet and read considerable newspapers of Abuja, Amsterdam, Brasilia, London, Paris, Pretoria, and Washington, before the early rising Nigerian farmers break their fast!

Granny had once recounted the revelation of *onifa inu iwe*, (his names mean the oracle of the book) the oracle of His Royal Majesty, the *alayeluwa,* the Ooni of ife, the city that witnesses first every dawn of the day. The old seer had recounted to the king what he saw or foresaw for that year. He had seen a giant grass cutter, speeding over an unusually wide path dyed completely black. The oracle man had witnessed the unusual: the giant rat was carrying inside it some human beings, suddenly turned turtle. Lo and behold, corpses were being extracted from the giant grass cutter.

The Holy scriptures are right: we see dimly as through a mirror. The oracle man, about the year 1900, had seen in parts future developments by then, yet to come to Nigeria. He had delineated the silhouette of tarred roads, and motor vehicles, road accidents with fatalities. The old medium got it but all wrong as he vowed to ensure that such deadly giant rats, say motor vehicles, should never meet him on the surface of the earth. He would not witness either dying black of wide bush paths, where giant bush rats would carry and kill humans inside them.

Femoo can't but pity the aged oracle man. He did not live to see the super golden eagle hatch. The old seer did not witness them grow electronic feathers, flap them and fan off every figment of prejudice, darkness, abuse and taboos.

While his preceding generation groped in the dark, Femoo's flew the jet age, watched man's giant stride on the moon and welcomed the advent of coloured films, videos, and mobile telephones. His children's generation went further by almost all standards. These young guys have simply metamorphosed into other beings. They cross continents by simply swinging on their swivel chairs. They merely push buttons and scale the digital divide that had kept their ancestors bound and victims of the evil forest of dark ages! But say, are speed and electronic chips the essence of humanity? Will these indeed change these kids and enlarge their souls to sow and tender the seeds of love and weed out the evil tares of the old nature?

And what more? They were blessed with a Baba who was able to convince creditors of their country's debt overhang to withdraw their sword and loose the noose hanging all. Now, they have the peace of mind to build a solid base for banks and bridges over all gaps. Their generation has all the choices to swing, sail or fly on the wings of times and spaces. But does their speed mean quick recovery from the fatal bite of immorality and remedy from the sickness of insensitivity to other people's sufferings?

It seems the whole of humanity has been flung into an ageless sea of turbulence, tension with tricks and traders of tackles. The options are still there in this world deadly battle of the sea. Some simply freeze their mind, resign, drink and drown alone. They are victims. Some free their minds, float, ferry themselves together, fish and flourish together. Some probe further, prospect, perceive and prime their minds under the great leader and teacher: The Truth. Then, they go ahead to control the tides and times. Today, both the truth and trade tend towards them.

If Femoo's generation was called liberals his children's are probably now "liberators of hope". He therefore finds it ridiculous, in fact senseless, that most generations of Nigeria tend to prevent the petals of their succeeding generations from opening. They try to overstay on the stage, even when the giver had withdrawn from their set the shine and staff of leadership. Many of them miss the praise of exiting at the loudest ovation and earn nothing but shame of a stranded star that tries to twinkle at noon time. Every dog must have its day. Everything has its time. It is the law of the Creator and His nature. In this world, the stars of the night must give way to the rising sun of a new dawn.

Of course, it is just as Prophet Daniel was warned that knowledge would increase and that he should go his way.

"But go thou thy way till the end be: for thou shalt rest, and stand in thy lot at the end of the days". The Holy Bible, Daniel chapter 12, verse 13.

In the same way, all generations, willy-nilly, as well as Femoo and his generation will go their way. His children and their generation will probably rush, fly or surf theirs.

Till then, will they halt or hold or help in hoping? Or will they be probing or prospecting for their own tide turner so that the wings and swings of times and tides may tend also towards them?

Time may tell.

Femoo paced up and down under the flamboyant tree. He shook his head and wiped the beads of sweat with his Chinese handkerchief.

He finally sat on the exposed roots and kept shaking his head. The sweat welled up again.

'Dad, are you ok? You're sweating! His daughter pointing at him.

'Darling, 'am ok. This time he got his local flannel face towel. His face was wiped clean. He can enjoy the breeze from his clean shaved head to the sole of his feet.

Life after all, is an adventure. It may be sweet; it may be sour. It may lift you up and it may sometimes knock you down. It may be amazing. What will be will be. *Que sara sara*
. But as the Yoruba say, *eni ti egungun ba n lee, ko maa roju bi o se n re ara aye bee naa ni o n re ara orun.* If you are pursued by masquerade, you just must keep running just as humans get tired, so do masquerades too.

The important thing is to keep running.

Glossary of words

Chapter 1

Iroko: hard wood tree found usually on the tropics, botanical name is Milicia excelsa;
Oja: swaddling cloth or sash to strap babies on the back, a common practice in Nigeria.
egusi:melon seed ground as stew with vegetables
Baale: the village head
owe: Proverbs
ada oyinbo: here, machete of the white man, being industrial machete as opposed to the cheaper and less efficient local blacksmith's
Eba: Meal made of grated and dried cassava, called garri, soaked in boiled water. The paste realized is the meal
oriki:eulogies or praise names,among the Yorubas, it recounts also, the ancient exploits of a person's ancestors.
mama onile: the land lady

Chapter 2
Igbo Olose:the Olose forest.
"Aje! Aje", Yoruba word meaning, "witch! Witch!"

Chapter 3
1.Petesi:a storey building.
2. Ile alaja, Yoruba words for a storey building.
3. okan omo eniyan: the soul or heart of man
4. Esu: Satan
5. ofada or alabere: two species of rice, the former grain being more robust
6. Bata: Yoruba drum, spindle chordophone, famous for its stammering rhythm and danced to violently.

Chapter 4

aadun:a type of local cake baked on hot,open basin from dry maize grain.

misisi: local way of addressing the school mistress.

 Ijoko Idera: which is, "sitting at ease" It is a painful posture of punishment by which pupils would sit on bare floor with their legs and arms raised up.

4.Kokoro wuye, wuye, wuye: 'wriggling insect, wriggling, wriggling'.

5. esunsun or zinge in the north. Winged termites, that usually fly around lamps in June, every year.

6. Garri: is grated, dried cassava tuber, used for various meals in West Africa and Latin America.

7. Paripa: goliath beetle. The male has horn like that of the rhinoceros while the female does not.

Chapter 5

ose ero ree o: here comes popular soap; locally made black but rich soap.

amala a deep brown or outright black meal from yam or plantain flour.

alo: fables,moon light tales, the night stories.

Yanibo: the bittle, the wife of the tortoise in Yoruba fables

Chapter 6

1. eko: maize or corn meal, solid pap usually wrapped in leaves

Chapter 7

bolekaja: wooden passenger lorry, the name actually means, 'come down and let's settle it with a fight'.

Gbago: simple but broad and luxuriant leaves growing in tropical marshy areas.

ajeku ekun: the left over from the tiger.

Chapter 8

"E gba mi o": Please save me! Or please help.

Graded questions on chapters 1 to 14

Chapter 1

In the Beginning

What efforts were made to capture Femoo?
Where was Femoo at the beginning of this book?
How did Femoo show his anger?
  Why was he in this situation?
  What is the elder's court?
Why does he like to stay on the farm? How is Alapata?
  How do you build sand castles?
Who is Ojo?
  What are proverbs and why do they confuse Femoo?

Chapter 2

The Warriors

 What is a Greek gift foisted on the Christ Apostolic
Church people?
Why did Olu drink Kerosene?
 Describe how Olu was revived
 Who were the warriors fighting?
What is blessed water and what can it do?
Why was Simi so fast asleep? How was she woken up?
Why did the witches refuse to eat up Olu?

Chapter 3

A Night Out

Who is Baba?
Describe his house
What is a jackpot? How did Femoo win or lose his?
How did Femoo's first telephone conversation go?
How did the boys enjoy their night time in bed?
'The fear of daddy is the beginning of wisdom'. Discuss.
Explain: 'there was more threat than thrashing'
What are questions of life as against life of questions?
Describe the sleeping pattern of Femoo's home.
What is an elephant's head?
Explain smacking of lips during thunder storms.
What makes Sundays special
How will Femoo like his soul to be?
Describe the two methods of preparing rice for cooking?
Why does Femoo prefer pounded yam to rice?

Chapter 4

School Begins

Why was young Femoo snatched from Granny's caring hand?
Why did Femoo prefer uncle Afe to uncle Osu?
What was Femoo's 'Plan for Freedom'?
How was the test for children of school age?
Explain why some pupils kept their father's name secret?
Why did uncle Osu lay ambush? How did Femoo enjoy the school environment?
Why was the Oldsmobile parked in front of Baba Lambert's house?
Describe the inspector's quarters. What is the school routine?
Describe two types of punishment inflicted on erring pupils.

The English class was demonstrative. How?

Why were drawings or music classes introduced during rains?

How did the school teach pupils to: a) protect insects; b) safe their time?

Why was arithmetic the enemy number one? Explain the big arithmetic question on Femoo's mind.

What is 'kokoro wuye,wuye,wuye'?

Who taught Femoo to catch locust? Describe the two methods of catching insects for meals?

Explain the link between insects, toads and snakes. Why are toads dangerous at night?

Describe Itamarun. How was the bridge built and often swept away?

Who was the strange weaver? Why did Femoo fear him so much?

How did the weaver die? Do you think Femoo is a prophet?

What happened to Femoo on 6/6/66?

Chapter 5

Dinner on the Farm

What do you think is behind Granny's special love for Femoo?

Describe 'baby'. How did it die? how does granny get rid of rats?

What gave Olu a bloody finger?

Mention two methods of hunting by boys on the farm. How was the game shared?

Describe the puppies' game at home.

Describe Obi's workshop. What could boys play with there?

How was dinner on the farm? Describe the night stories scene with granny.

How did the monkey finally learn to say 'amen'?

What danger was there with the pirates in granny's time?

Who was Baba Isobo's father? How did he die?
How did Femoo's grandpa buy the Baba Isobo's ancestor?
What is an iguana?

Chapter 6

What's up in Town?

What is a triangular walk?
What side shows are there in town?
Who are Yemi, and Kanbi ?
How is 'eko' prepared?
What is 'Ajuruna' and who made it?
The headmaster was a rather shrewd man. Describe the brick-making factory of the pupils.
How did the school Principal come to know all the pupil's names on the first day at school?
Why couldn't Femoo's uncle help pay his school fees?
Femoo's dad was a great genius, explain.
The Cooperative society was Femoo's salvation. Do you agree?
How was Femoo's first trip to Lagos?
The Lagos metropolitan life style breads insensitivity and kills African culture. Illustrate with a few examples.

Chapter 7

Too armed to judge Here!
Describe the approach to Alapata.
Who is uncle Lemuel? Why does he limp?
What does the story of baby Lemuel's close shave with death teach you about the old rural life at Ife?
Why was Femoo invited to the elders' council?
Describe the powerful weapons of the two thieves.

Why could the village elders not judge the thieves?
Do you think the thieves would get justice in town?

Chapter 8

The civil War days

Describe the assailants of Mama Barbara
What saved her?
Itemize three episodes of excesses of the Politicians
Describe briefly the scene preceding the civil war
State some measures taken by Femoo's father to protect his
house from enemy bombs.
How did Femoo's mother react to the news of the Biafran
propaganda?

Chapter 9

Dad's Death
When and where did Femoo's dad die?
How was the news of the death of Femoo's death broken to
him?
How could Granny tell that Femoo was bringing bad news?
How did mum cope with her widowhood?
What are considered as tell tale signs of hard-working
students?
Why did Femoo shed two types of tear?
What used to happen at Oke Oloyibo?
Explain the change of attitude of the Ife parents after the
civil war.

Chapter 10
The University
Give a brief description of the University of Ife when
Femoo first visited.
What is the d-day? Who is a JJC?

How did Femoo's mother prepare him for the University campus?

Explain: 'everyone for himself, devil takes the last man'.

Who were Sifawu and Abeni?

Give two examples of abuse of office by the university lecturer?

What is 'October rush'?

What did Femoo miss most on Sundays?

Chapter 11

In France

Give two advantages of studying French language in France?

What was the shocker that Femoo had on looking for a church nearby in France?

What is 'Ali Mon Go'?

How did Femoo's job interview go?

What were the fears of parents about the NYSC posting of their children?

How did Femoo enjoy his NYSC.

Chapter 12

Wild world of Gorillas

Why did one lecturer criticize the Foreign service?

Explain 'an unending jail term' feared by Femoo's wife.

Describe the menu for professional success and peace recommended by Femoo.

What was the undoing of the Difa gorillas?

Explain the story of the cock and the fox.

Chapter 13

The Havoc or Hope?

Explain the adoption of animals in the zoo.

'wherever the elephant faces is the way' explain

What do the young Femoos mean by the question' why are things like these?'

What is '99 standing and 20 sitting'?

Do you think uncle Olajuba was better educated than Femoo?

How can you explain what ravaged the zoo and Femoo's alma mater?

What is the nectar of new life?

What is the new land of hope?

Explain the revelation of Onifa Inu Iwe?

Compare the generation of Femoo to that of his children.

 What will be will be. Explain.

Who are the liberators of hope?

Advance Level Questions

Explain the roles of Proverbs and idiomatic expressions in this novel

Femoo is a typical African child do you agree?

In this novel, on the wings of Time, there seems to be an inextricable duel between the modern and the old, the rural and the urban life. Explain.

List instances of child abuse or inconsideration for children's rights in the traditional life of this novel.

What role do passage of time and travels play in development of the young Femoo?

What does the ultimate success of the hero teach us, today?

The novel, on the wings of Time is a masterpiece on grooming and traditional African hospitality. Do you agree?

Femoo in Larry Femi's novel, On the Wings of Time is a type of a struggling African child. Do you agree?

The beauty of fresh Mother Nature, flora and fauna is preponderant in this novel. Give instances.

Explain the type of police here from the scenes at the charge office.

What are Diffa Gorillas? What are their real challenges? Any way out for these endangered animals or are they doomed?

Femoo's bright hope of showcasing his alma mater to his children was suddenly dashed. What smoldered such a passion? What was his solution?

What are the factors that helped young Femoo to climb up in the social ladder?

The author's strong points include his masterful deployment of Yoruba proverbs and idiomatic expressions. Explain.

Larry Femi's book. Amazing Adventures of Femoo or On the Wing of Times is of great inspiration to the youth. Do you agree? The book encourages you to keep running. What does this mean?

Amazing Adventures of Femoo or On the wings of Time is a journey into the life of the Nigerian life. Do you agree?

Printed in Great Britain
by Amazon